"I will never set foot in this house again, I promise you."

Kellen stared at her for a full minute. She was magnificent. A lioness defending her lair. Except that it was *his* lair. And it was his hand that wanted to touch her trembling chin. His body that hungered to feel her passion. Her fire.

"Goddammit, Lolly."

"Goddammit what?" She spit the words at him, and all at once he couldn't stand it one more second. He kissed her.

Big, big tactical error. Her lips under his were like warm velvet. Suddenly he wanted his mouth, and his hands, on every inch of her skin.

"Stop," she said after a few exquisitely sensual explorations of her neck and throat. "Kellen, you must stop."

"Why must I?" he murmured against her hair. He kissed her again. He didn't want to stop. *Ever.*

* * *

The Wedding Cake War
Harlequin Historical #730—November 2004

LYNNA BANNING

THE WEDDING CAKE WAR

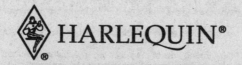

TORONTO • NEW YORK • LONDON
AMSTERDAM • PARIS • SYDNEY • HAMBURG
STOCKHOLM • ATHENS • TOKYO • MILAN • MADRID
PRAGUE • WARSAW • BUDAPEST • AUCKLAND

ISBN 0-373-29330-5

THE WEDDING CAKE WAR

Copyright © 2004 by The Woolston Family Trust

www.eHarlequin.com

Printed in U.S.A.

Available from Harlequin Historicals and
LYNNA BANNING

Western Rose #310
Wildwood #374
Lost Acres Bride #437
Plum Creek Bride #474
The Law and Miss Hardisson #537
The Courtship #613
The Angel of Devil's Camp #649
The Scout #682
High Country Hero #706
One Starry Christmas #723
"Hark the Harried Angels"
The Wedding Cake War #730

Please address questions and book requests to:
Harlequin Reader Service
U.S.: 3010 Walden Ave., P.O. Box 1325, Buffalo, NY 14269
Canadian: P.O. Box 609, Fort Erie, Ont. L2A 5X3

In memory of my mother,
Mary Elizabeth (Banning) Yarnes

With grateful thanks to Suzanne Barrett, Tricia Adams,
Debbie Parcel, Brenda Preston, Susan Renison,
David Woolston and Andrew Yarnes.

Chapter One

Oregon, 1879

If she'd thought about it for one single minute, Lolly would never have boarded the train in Kansas City. That was a character failing, she supposed—jumping headlong from the saucepan into the cook-fire. She'd inherited the tendency from her father.

Which was exactly why he was dead and she was breathing the cigar-smoky air of this railway coach. In all his forty years on this earth, Papa had never backed down, changed his opinion or avoided a fight.

And neither would she. With a bit of luck and some…well…acting ability, she would triumph over any adversity. Even marriage to a man she'd never laid eyes on.

The train slowed, then chuffed to a stop. "Maple Falls," the conductor shouted from the back of the car. "Home of sawmills, grist mills, gin mills, wild women and the Methodist church."

Lolly choked down a bubble of laughter. If only half those things were true, Maple Falls would prove intriguing. In a town with both Shady Ladies, as Pa had termed them, and Our Heavenly Father's Second-Best Parlor, as her Presbyterian mother dubbed the Methodist church, there was the promise of happenings that might prove interesting. She most fervently hoped so. After her impulsive flight from Baxter Springs, she badly needed some cheering up.

Lolly bit the inside of her lip. She needed more than cheering up. She needed a new life. A new place, as far from Kansas as she could get. She only hoped it wasn't too late.

At the thought, her entire body turned to petrified whalebone. She was too outspoken, too set in her ways. Too plump.

Too…old.

Maybe it *was* too late.

Get off the train, a voice commanded. *Just put one foot in front of the other and walk out into Oregon.*

It was harder than she anticipated. For one thing,

her fancy new jab-toed shoes, ordered from Bloomingdale's, pinched her feet. And for another, all at once she felt as if her bottom half was glued to the seat; every bone in her body resisted moving a single step toward the momentous event that awaited her. She could scarcely breathe she was so frightened.

The coach emptied, and still Lolly sat stiff as chicken wire on the hard leather seat until a head poked into the far end of the car.

"Miz Mayfield?"

She sucked a gulp of smoky air into her lungs. "Yes?"

"Better hurry up, ma'am. Train's about to pull out."

As the boy spoke, the railcar jerked and began to glide forward.

Good gracious! Which was worse, being inadvertently kidnapped by a train, or facing a town full of hungry lions? Well, maybe not lions, exactly. But she knew exactly how the Christian martyrs in Roman arenas must have felt. Trapped.

Lolly stood up, grasped her leather satchel and made her way unsteadily up the aisle, clinging to the backs of the seats until she reached the iron debarking step.

The train engine tooted twice and began to accelerate.

"Jump, ma'am! Hurry, it's rollin'."

Jump? Was he crazy? She'd break both her ankles in these shoes.

She heaved the satchel into the young man's arms and hurriedly unsnapped one French kid boot, then the other, tossing them out the train door just as the coach began to pick up speed. Wrapping her knitted wool shawl about her head, she folded her arms over her chest, whispered a quick prayer and stepped off the platform.

She toppled into the youth clasping her satchel, knocking him flat onto the wood platform. His wide-brimmed hat rolled away under the spinning train wheels.

"Godalmighty, ma'am, whadja do that for?"

Lolly sat up, straightened her black straw bonnet and scooted her knees off the young man's chest. "To get off the train, of course. You said to jump."

"Sufferin' scorpions, ma'am, I didn't mean on top of me!"

Lolly rose to a standing position, her legs shaking like twin columns of jelly. Her stocking-covered toes curled against the uneven boards beneath her feet, telling her where every splinter lurked in the rough wood. What a way to begin her new life, making a spectacle of herself in public.

She scanned the onlookers. Was *he* here? Watching her stumble about like a tipsy Presbyterian? *Would he change his mind when he saw her?*

She bent over the boy. "I am extremely sorry. Are you hurt?"

"Heck, no, I ain't hurt." He assessed her generous figure. "I guess I've been hit by hay bales bigger'n—" His voice trailed off.

"Beg pardon, Miz Mayfield. You ain't shaped like no bale of hay, no matter how—" His thin face flushed the color of cooked beets.

Lolly took pity on him. "Have you a name, young man?"

"Huh? Oh, sure. But at the moment I can't exactly recall— Oh yeah, it's Henry Morehouse, ma'am. At your service."

Lolly suppressed a burst of laughter. "Well, Henry Morehouse, I am Leora Mayfield." She extended her hand. "I have been in correspondence with the ladies here in town, and I have come out from Kansas to marry—"

"Oh, we know all about that, Miz Mayfield." He hoisted her travel satchel in one hand and offered his arm. "I'll escort you over to the schoolhouse to get registered."

"Schoolhouse? Isn't there a hotel?"

"Why, sure, ma'am. We'll get you registered there, too."

She peered at him. He was a nice-looking, lanky boy of about fifteen, she guessed. Clear-blue eyes and floppy wheat-colored hair.

"Why must I register at the schoolhouse?"

As her question sank in, his cheeks colored. "Well, you see, ma'am, the colonel, he figured... well, he figured—"

"Colonel! Mr. Macready is a colonel? In what army, may I ask?"

"He was a Reb, ma'am. But not anymore. War's been over some years now."

"I am aware of that." She brushed off her skirt, keeping her head down so her black straw bonnet shielded her face. So, Mr. Macready had been a Confederate soldier. Papa had fought on the Union side. Her saucepan was boiling over.

"What," she said in as steady a voice as she could manage, "precisely *has* the colonel 'figured'?"

"That you all could sign up at the schoolhouse first. That way, we'll know how many."

She tried hard not to frown, she really did. Frowning just added wrinkles to her already sun-dried face. Not that anyone knew how parched her skin was; no one but herself ever touched her cheek or her nose, or any other part of her. Which was the reason why she was braving the wilds of Oregon instead of withering into an old maid in Kansas.

"That way you'll know how many *what?*"

Henry Morehouse studied his dusty brown button-top shoes. "I'd rather not say, Miz Mayfield. Best we just go along and do it. You'll find out soon enough."

"Henry?" Back in Kansas, grown men had quaked at that tone. She used it now because she was exasperated.

The boy shuffled two steps backward. "Don't usually answer to Henry," he mumbled. "My friends call me Hank."

Lolly stepped toward him. In her stocking feet they were exactly the same height. "Hank, then. Best we just 'go along and do' what?"

"S-sign up, ma'am. Like I told ya."

"Sign up for what?" She narrowed her eyes in her best Pin the Polecat look and watched the Morehouse boy bite his lower lip.

"For, uh…for what the colonel figured, ma'am. That's all I can tell ya, till we get to the school-house."

Lolly spun on her heel, then wished she hadn't.

Ignoring the bite of wood splinters through her stocking, she collected her shoes from the platform, rescued Hank's mashed hat from the railroad tracks and returned to the motionless boy.

"March," she ordered.

"Oh, yes, ma'am." He started to salute, then realized his error and grinned sheepishly at her. "Just follow me."

The schoolhouse sat smack in the center of a field of blue lupine and scarlet Indian paintbrush. A wandery path snaked its way through the ankle-deep blooms to a run-down building that looked more dilapidated than any farmer's neglected barn in Kansas. Why, the gaps between the split logs weren't even chinked! She could tell they had been at one time, but the mud-and-straw daubing had dissolved to dust. The wind, or the snow, could whistle through at will. No doubt the students froze in the winter and baked in the summer.

It was high summer now, Lolly reflected as she zigzagged along the path behind Hank Morehouse. The air brushing her cheeks felt hot, and the heavy, lazy heat pressed the air out of her lungs. The schoolhouse would be an oven.

And it was. The instant she stepped over the threshold her already-wilting underclothes stuck to her back and chest, and her muslin drawers pasted themselves to her legs. At every step she heard the *skitch-skitch* of her inner thighs brushing together. Could everyone else hear it, too?

The three gray-haired ladies seated behind a long oak table didn't even look up. The only other occupants of the room were two younger women sitting off to one side, spines straight, hands folded, smiles unwavering.

Lolly crossed the uneven plank floor with a sinking feeling in the pit of her stomach. Was this some sort of inquisition?

Hank clumped up to the table. "Got another one fer ya." He plopped her satchel on top of an empty school desk and stuffed his lanky frame into the child-size seat.

All three elderly women snapped their heads up.

Lolly's stomach tightened into a hard knot. *Another* one? Another *what?*

A large-bosomed matron in a royal-blue day dress grasped a pencil. "Name?"

"Another what?" Lolly ventured in her Refined Voice.

The woman's eyebrows waggled. "Bride," she said. A satisfied smile spread over her face. "Name?"

"Leora Mayfield." Lolly swallowed. "But I believe I am the *only* bride. At least that was my understanding from the newspaper advertisement.''

"Oh, no, dearie," a lilting voice sang. "There's no profit in just *one* bride."

"Profit?"

"Well, you see, dearie," the woman cooed. "We, that is the Maple Falls Ladies Helpful Society, are determined to finance construction of a new schoolhouse. You can see for yourself that this one is in such sad disrepair, and—"

"Let me tell it, Minnie." The Bosom in Royal Blue made a sweeping gesture. "This schoolhouse was built back in twenty-seven, you see, when old Abel Svensen left us a small bequest in his will."

"That was over fifty years ago," Minnie interjected, her hands fluttering as she spoke. Dressed in a lavender-sprigged dimity, the tiny woman looked like a dainty butterfly trying to decide where to land.

"Now," Royal Blue continued, "the walls are collapsing, the floor is buckling, the outhouse needs—"

"Dora Mae Landsfelter!" Minnie's hands danced. "Not in polite company."

Dora Mae turned snapping blue eyes on Lolly. "So you see, Miss Mayfield, that is why we need a new schoolhouse."

"But..."

"Why," the older woman continued in a no-nonsense tone, "we, the ladies of the Maple Falls Helpful Society, have resolved to raise the necessary funds." She held Lolly's gaze in an unblinking look.

"Why," chimed the third woman, rising from her chair behind the table, "the Helpful Ladies are sponsoring this competition."

Lolly blinked at the three. "Competition?"

"To be the bride!" Minnie's hands swooped and circled in the warm air. "Isn't it exciting?"

Exciting? Lolly pondered the word. Being a bride would certainly be exciting. The answer to her prayers. All her life she'd longed to fall in love and marry, have a family, a home of her own. Now, as she approached her thirtieth year of virginity, she'd given up on the fall-in-love part. She just wanted to get married and have a family, like other women.

But a competition?

"What kind of competition?" She tried to use her Kansas Quaking voice, to no avail.

The lace ruffles at Minnie's neck shuddered with excitement. "Oh, dearie, I'm so glad you inquired. Our competition—"

"Let me tell it," Dora Mae interrupted. "First, the candidates will—"

"*I* thought up that part," the third woman chirped. "Let *me* tell it!"

"Candidates?" Lolly whispered. *Candidates?*

"Of course," Dora Mae exclaimed. "What is a competition without competitors? Ruth, you didn't make that part at all clear."

Ruth Underwood's round, pleasant face fell. "Oh, of course, the competitors." She tipped her head toward the two young women seated against the wall. "Miss LeClair just arrived yesterday. And—"

Dora Mae raised an admonishing hand and took over. "And our own hometown candidate is Miss Gundersen. She's the schoolteacher, so we thought…"

Minnie's hands took flight. "We selected our schoolteacher to represent all the other women in Maple Falls, the ones who—"

"Who have been pursuing our prize bachelor, Colonel Macready, for years. The ladies of the Helpful Society thought it best to avoid infighting among our native population."

Lolly needed to sit down. Her head spun, and her undergarments were beginning to feel squishy against her hot skin. Worst of all, she wanted to laugh. Papa always said if something funny went by, notice it. Well, now she was noticing it like crazy. This whole idea was ludicrous.

She had been duped. She'd sold the newspaper office and vacated her room at the boardinghouse in Baxter Springs and come out to Oregon to… to…well, not to marry, as it turned out. To compete for the groom!

It was too much. Simply beyond the pale.

At that moment a disturbing idea flitted into her consciousness. "What is wrong with Colonel Macready?"

Three pairs of eyes widened in consternation. Dora Mae's pencil catapulted out of her fingers and clicked onto the floor. "Wrong?"

"Oh, dearie, you can't be serious?" Minnie fanned her face with her fingers.

"That man is God's gift to the feminine gender," Ruth added. "Why, even my old heart quakes something terrible when he as much as walks by, and I've been—"

"Married for thirty-four years," Minnie finished for her.

"Thirty-five years, Min. Makes no difference. That man is a *man*."

"I see," Lolly said. "And we, the three of us—" she glanced at the two young women now perched at the edge of their chairs ''—are supposed to...''

She couldn't say it. Something inside her rebelled at the thought of having to compete for a husband. By all rights, in a civilized world, it should be the other way around. *He* should fight for *her*. After all, Cinderella did not chase after the prince, did she?

On the other hand, Cinderella wasn't counting the days until her thirtieth birthday. A lump of hot coal plopped into her chest.

Lolly's gaze traveled over the trio of Helpful Ladies to rest briefly on Hank Morehouse, slumped in decided disinterest over her satchel, his eyes shut. She forced her attention to the other two candidates.

Both young. Twenty at the most. One, dressed in a stylishly cut emerald-green silk with matching shoes and a fringed parasol, looked the perfect Southern lady. Miss LeClair, no doubt. Even in the wilting heat, not one hair straggled from her crown of golden ringlets.

The other woman, seated next to Miss LeClair, looked even younger in a pretty blue-checked gingham with pearl buttons all the way to the hem. Her soulful brown eyes were set in a rather plain-featured face.

Lolly knew exactly what had driven herself to this step. What, she wondered, was wrong with *them?*

Perhaps, a voice whispered, *they are as desperate as you are.*

She eyed the younger women again. Both held her gaze for a brief moment, and in that instant Lolly recognized something. Whatever their reasons, whatever their differences, they were all sisters under the skin. They all wanted to get married.

"It's for the school, dearie. You do see that, don't you?" Minnie's sugary voice floated to her over the buzzing in her ears.

"For the children," Dora Mae added. "Twenty-seven students will attend the Maple Falls school come the fall term. They simply must have a new—"

"All right, all right," Lolly murmured. "A schoolhouse is a fine thing in a community."

Dora Mae thrust the pencil at her. "Just sign right here, Miss Mayfield."

"And then," sang Minnie, her hands stroking the air, "you can meet the other brides."

Chapter Two

Dora Mae smoothed the creases in her royal-blue skirt, captured Lolly's hand and tugged her across the floor. "May I introduce Miss Fleurette LeClair, from New Orleans. Miss Leora Mayfield."

The green-silk-clad woman tipped her head. Her face wasn't the least bit welcoming. It wasn't even friendly. Her green eyes shot ice chips up and down Lolly's plain black travel ensemble. Lolly tried to smile.

The perfect lips opened. "Wheah you from?"

"Um…well, I'm from Baxter Springs, Kansas. I used to run a news—"

"Oh," Miss LeClair sniffed. "That explains it."

Lolly's mouth opened of its own accord. "Explains what?"

"All that black," Fleurette drawled. "And, my heavens, yoah shoes."

"What's wrong with my shoes? They're brand-new. I ordered them from Bloom—"

"It's summertime, honey. Or have you not noticed?"

"And this," Minnie interrupted with a flutter in her voice, "is Miss Careen Gundersen. Most everyone calls her Carrie, and she was born and raised right here in Maple Falls."

Carrie extended her hand and enfolded Lolly's in a firm grasp. "I don't in the least object to black in the summer," she murmured. "It's quite elegant."

Lolly smiled at her, then turned her gaze to include Miss LeClair. "I am pleased to meet you both, even under these rather odd circumstances."

Her remark met with a prolonged silence.

"I mean, it *is* a bit odd, don't you think? All three of us competing for the same—"

"Decidedly," Miss LeClair acknowledged with a little nod that made her ringlets bounce.

"Perhaps just a bit," Carrie allowed. "But you haven't met Colonel Macready yet. He—" she drew the word out on a long sigh "—makes it all worthwhile."

"Really," murmured Miss LeClair.

Carrie beamed. "I've been calculating the odds.

I'm quite good at mathematics, being a school-teach…''

Her voice trailed off as Miss LeClair pivoted and headed for the doorway, unfurling her parasol on the way.

"I am not interested in mathematical odds," she said over her shoulder. "It is a lady's breedin' and accomplishments that will tip the scale."

Her cool-as-silk tone hinted at an assumed superiority that made Lolly's lips tighten. The back of her neck began to tingle. For a fleeting moment she imagined a jungle, tangled green vines full of twittering birds and silent, deadly snakes. Deep inside her a kill-or-be-killed instinct stirred.

Carrie broke the awkward quiet. "Let's all go over to the hotel and have some lemonade, shall we?" Her earnest brown eyes rested on Lolly, then on Miss LeClair. Lolly watched Fleurette deliberately turn her back and address the Helpful Ladies.

"When am Ah to meet Colonel Macready?"

The older women looked at one another. "This afternoon," Dora Mae replied.

"This evening," Ruth said in the same instant.

Minnie's hands swooped in front of her face. "Well, we hadn't exactly decided when…."

Miss LeClair's parasol spun to a halt. "This evening, Ah take it. And what will be the occasion?

Ah ask because Ah wish to dress appropriately.''
She cast a disparaging glance at Lolly's traveling
costume, then lingered on Carrie's blue check.
''Did you make that yourself?'' she inquired.

''Why, yes. I sew quite a bit and…''

''Exactly,'' came the murmured response. ''Ah
thought as much.''

That tone of voice, Lolly thought, was like the
hiss of a poisonous viper. Rarely had she taken
such an instant dislike to another human being, unless it was a braggadocio Rebel soldier exulting
over some past victory or attacking her latest newspaper editorial.

Lady or not, Miss Green Eyes from New Orleans
was just plain rude. And stuck-up. It would be pure
pleasure to take some of the starch out of her no-
doubt perfectly stiff petticoats.

Carrie just smiled. ''Come on. I calculate it to
be ninety-seven degrees in here. Doesn't a glass of
cold lemonade sound just about perfect? It will
lower our body temperature at least two degrees.''

Lolly guessed there wasn't a mean bone in Carrie's slim, gingham-swathed body or her fact-
overloaded brain. She might be a little pedantic,
but that was because she was a trained teacher.

Lolly was educated, too. She had read her way
through the Baxter Springs library shelves while

she struggled to keep the newspaper going so she could care for her mother. Her education might have been a bit sporadic, but who cared if she'd discovered Shakespeare before she stumbled onto Plato?

Besides, she reasoned, there wasn't one of the occupants in this musty-smelling schoolroom who couldn't stand to learn something new. Herself included.

Lemonade sounded like a fine place to start.

"Do tell us, Miss Gundersen, Ah mean, Carrie, what do you know of Colonel Macready?" Fleurette swirled another teaspoonful of sugar into her lemonade glass.

Lolly watched Carrie's heart-shaped face come alive at the mention of the man's name. With such a pronounced case of hero worship, she wondered how the young woman could stomach having two rivals sipping cold drinks at the same table.

"Oh, the colonel is…well, he is just wonderful. Simply, truly…wonderful."

"Wonderful," Fleurette echoed dryly. She tapped her spoon against the edge of her glass and laid it on the tiny pink tea napkin provided. "Wonderful, *how?*"

"Oh, in every way, I assure you. I've known

him all my life, you see. He came to live here in Maple Falls when I was four...or was I five? Let's see, I am nineteen now, and the colonel arrived right after the war. That's sixty-five subtracted from seventy-nine.... Yes, I was five. I remember it was on my birthday.''

''More to the point, how old is *he?*''

Carrie giggled. ''Oh, I calculate he's old enough to be my father and then some. But Dora Mae Landsfelter is years younger than her husband, and she said such things don't matter in the least.''

''Carrie,'' Lolly said, her voice gentle. ''Could you calculate how old the colonel is *exactly.*''

Carrie closed her soft brown eyes for a moment. ''Forty-three.''

Fleurette lifted her lips away from her lemonade. ''Ah do wonder why he has not married in all this time.''

Lolly's hand stilled on her glass. The question had occurred to her, as well. How *had* the town's prize catch remained uncaught for fourteen years?

''Well,'' Carrie began, lowering her voice, ''some people say he lost a sweetheart in the war and never recovered. Others say he's stubborn and set in his ways and he never before wanted a wife for fear she'd change him.''

Lolly's ears burned. Stubborn? Set in his ways?

The same had been said of her ever since she turned fourteen.

"He hardly lets anyone female into his house," Carrie went on, "except for old Mrs. Squires. She's kept house for him for years, but the colonel does all his own cooking, and Mrs. Squires says he even irons his own shirts. Can you imagine?"

"If he married, he would require servants," Fleurette murmured. "Ah have had servants all my life."

Lolly bit her tongue. Slaves, more likely. She squashed down a ripple of anger and decided to change the subject. "What is his home like?"

"It's a big white house with gray shutters, and it has three whole floors and a music room and a library. I've never seen the library, but once I attended a recital in the—"

Fleurette cut her off. "Why would a bachelor purchase such a mansion?"

"Oh, he didn't purchase it. He inherited it from his great-aunt Henrietta on his father's side. She married a Northerner and came out west, but she died of the quinsy soon after the war.... Why, what's the matter, Leora? You look like you've seen a ghost."

Lolly unclenched the fist she hid in her lap. Mama had died of the quinsy a month after Papa had been killed at Chancellorsville. She spoke over a tightened throat. "Nothing is the matter."

"Do Ah understand that Colonel Macready is a Southerner?" The excitement was evident in Fleurette's voice.

"Oh, yes, he's a real Southern gentleman. From Virginia. He has the most courtly manners, when he wants to, that is. And he's so tall and well formed and..." Carrie blushed and gulped her lemonade.

"Why—" Fleurette paused, pinning her gaze on Carrie "—since you seem obviously smitten with the gentleman, has he never courted you?"

Carrie gaped at her. "Me! Every single female in this town, and even some not so single, are smitten with Colonel Macready. He's never courted *any* of us!"

"Perhaps because he is a Southerner, and y'all are Yankees," Fleurette murmured.

"Or perhaps," Lolly said in a level tone, "because he wants to be the Smitten and not the Smittee. So to speak."

Carrie gave a whoop of laughter and clapped her hand over her mouth, then continued. Lolly watched the green-eyed, golden-haired Fleurette straighten her spine and crook her little finger into a dainty arc.

"Ah'm sure that is exactly right, Miss…Maypole. A gentleman's heart is not easily won."

"Mayfield. It's Mayfield."

"Why, of course it is," Fleurette purred.

"In this case," Lolly continued, "the gentleman is willing to donate his heart to finance a schoolhouse. Apparently he doesn't care one way or the other whether he's smitten or not."

Fleurette tipped her head to one side like a curious robin. "We'll have to wait and see about that, now won't we?"

Carrie's hand drifted down from her mouth. "It won't matter, ladies. The colonel has given his word on the matter. He will marry whichever one of us wins the competition. Oh, I do hope it will be me!"

"Why, my dear, Ah'd say you are enamored of the gentleman."

"Actually," Carrie said. "I don't really know him very well. I'm just one of dozens of females in town who adore him and simply swoon when he smiles. But he treats us all exactly the same."

A calculating look came into Fleurette's eyes. "You don't know the first thing about this man, do you? Except that you swoon when he smiles."

"Why, no," Carrie said. "If I did, I'd surely tell you both. We're all in this together, are we not?"

"Precisely," Fleurette said, her voice light.

Lolly didn't like her tone, pleasant as Fleurette had tried to make it. Again, the back of her neck tingled.

The scent of the young woman's perfume, something cloyingly sweet and heavy, like gardenias, made Lolly's head swim. She turned away to draw an untainted breath and spied young Hank Morehouse lounging in the dining room doorway, sending hand signals in her direction. *Satchel. Upstairs. Room 3.*

Lolly nodded. No sooner had the boy disappeared than a blur of royal blue sateen announced the presence of Dora Mae Landsfelter.

"Ah, here you are," she trumpeted. "I have an announcement." Dora Mae clasped her hand over her still-heaving bosom. "This evening, at eight o'clock..." She panted.

The three candidates froze, fingers curled around their lemonade glasses.

"The Helpful Ladies will host a reception in the hotel ballroom. And at that time..." She paused dramatically. "You will meet Colonel Macready. She slanted a look at Fleurette. "Dress will be ladies' evening attire."

Fleurette gasped. "My trunks! Have they arrived?"

"They have. Mrs. Petrov had all three moved up to your room at her boardinghouse."

Lolly sat stricken, unable to move. Trunk? Her trunk had been on the train; in her agitation about disembarking she'd completely forgotten about it. Now she realized all her possessions, except for what she obviously carried in her travel satchel—clean undergarments and a shawl and her toiletries and her Bible—were still on the train and headed for Portland.

How could she have been so scatterbrained? All she had to wear this evening was the black faille traveling suit, which at this moment felt heavier—and hotter—than ever before. She desperately needed something light and airy. Something summery and man-catching, with flounces and ruffles and...

What in heaven's name could she do? Borrow something?

Don't be a goose. Both Carrie and Fleurette had slim, girlish proportions, while she... Well, she was as rounded as a model in a Rubens painting, her hips and bosom blooming generously above and below her tightly laced-in waist. Besides, the smug expression on Fleurette's perfect pink-and-cream face was enough to squash any such idea.

Carrie leaned toward her. "You look white as a huck towel," she whispered.

"I am trying to think," Lolly whispered back.

Carrie patted her hand. "You didn't bring trunks full of gowns like Fleurette, did you?"

Lolly shook her head. She'd die before she confessed to being so addlepated at the train station. She finished off her lemonade to shore up her spirits. Between now and eight o'clock she had to come up with a fairy godmother, or else something she could turn into a—

"Of course!" she said aloud.

"You've thought of something?" Relief edged Carrie's tone.

Would it be too daring?

"What is it? Oh, do tell me!"

It *would* be daring, Lolly decided. Outrageous, in fact. But, with her trunk rolling toward Portland, she had no choice.

She squeezed Carrie's small hand. "I will wear…black. That's all I can tell you at the moment."

Lolly unpacked the contents of her satchel, stripped down to her camisole and drawers, and began to experiment. Her two-piece travel dress hung on hangers at the window, the plain gored skirt rippling in the breeze and the separate buttoned jacket turning this way and that as if undecided which direction to face. Already the creases were disappearing from the tight-woven fabric.

She sponged off her sticky body, then stretched out on the blue bed quilt to assess the situation.

The room was spartan but tidy. The mirror over the matching bureau reflected the white china ewer and basin she'd used for her sponge bath; her Bible lay next to the fluted glass lamp.

The tall cherry armoire opposite the bed confronted her accusingly, waiting to be filled. But she had nothing to put in it but her nightgown and one clean petticoat.

How, *how?* could she start a new life with one black dress and a Bible? The Heavenly Father had done it in six days, but He was God. She was a mere mortal, and female at that.

And more frightened than she had ever been in her life. No one could possibly know how the turmoil in her brain or the twitters in her stomach made her lightheaded and nauseous. Setting columns of type, even under a tight deadline, was easy compared to dressing up, especially when one had nothing to dress up *in.* Even protecting her printing press with her father's revolver when her abolitionist editorials riled up the townspeople paled in

comparison to the terror she felt at meeting Colonel
Macready and the rest of the Maple Falls citizenry
in nothing but her plain black dress, a bit of imagination and a lot of daring.

She donned her long black skirt, then lifted the
black Spanish lace shawl from its tissue-paper nest
in her satchel and approached the mirror. Tucking
one edge of the delicate lace into the top of her
camisole, she wound the long ends around her
body, leaving her shoulders exposed. At her cleav-
age, she formed a soft knot and let the shawl fringe
dangle.

There. It looked…exotic. *Risqué.*

Elegant. *Sinful.*

Dear Lord in heaven, what if they arrested her?

Chapter Three

Kellen Macready's hand shook so violently he had to laugh. This evening's ordeal would be worse than Chickamauga.

He stepped to the door in his paneled mahogany bedroom and yanked it open. "Madge!"

A faint voice floated from the floor below. "What is it, Colonel? I'm rollin' out some biscuits."

Kellen groaned. Mrs. Squires's biscuits came out of the oven hard as minié balls. "I can't tie this damned neckpiece."

Footsteps clumped up the staircase. "Mercy me, you're worse than a bairn." Her rounded form appeared in the doorway, hands on her hips.

"Bairns don't wear neckpieces," he retorted. "Or shirts starched so stiff they crackle." He liked teasing Mrs. Squires. She wasn't afraid to talk back to him.

"I starch 'em the same way every week." She fussed at his neck, her knobbed fingers still dexterous in spite of her arthritis. "Why the devil are ye wearin' this fancied-up thingamabob tonight?"

"Because," Kellen gritted out, "I gave my word to Dora Mae Landsfelter."

"Oh, aye." Mrs. Squires's graying eyebrows drew together. "I remember. Sorry now, are ye?"

Kellen thought for a moment. "Only about the starch, Madge. I gave my word of honor about the rest. It will be all right in the end."

The housekeeper sniffed. "You hope."

Kellen jerked. He *did* hope. Then for the thousandth time in the past week he wondered how he'd gotten himself into this fix.

He'd considered marriage once, before the Great War and his twenty-first birthday. She'd wait for him, she said. But she hadn't. She married his best friend the spring he marched off with the Army of Virginia, and the next winter she succumbed to typhoid. Women laced their fingers around one's heart and then threw it away.

His intent was to keep his pledge to the school building fund committee, help them raise money. But he'd resolved that Dora Mae's harebrained scheme wouldn't involve any part of his heart. Plenty of people did not marry for love.

Mrs. Squires eyed him. "Are you absolutely sure you want to do this?"

"Reasonably sure, yes. For one thing, it will put a stop to that gaggle of matchmaking mothers pushing their daughters at me. And their sisters and their widowed aunts and their cousins and..."

Besides, he was the last male in the Macready line. He would hate to pass from this world without leaving an heir.

And in addition, you damned fool, you gave Mrs. Landsfelter your word.

Underneath he knew there was more to it than Dora Mae's persuasive powers. Lately he'd been hungry for something more in his life. Something to fill the void yawning before him as he grew yet another year older. It was the one thing Kellen could not admit to anyone else. He was lonely. He wanted someone to talk to. Someone to laugh with.

Lolly's heart plunked into her stomach like a bucket full of rocks. The receiving line stretched from the ballroom entrance halfway around the huge ballroom to the cloth-covered refreshment table, a distance of maybe twenty feet. To her, it seemed like the Great Wall of China.

And all those people!

She liked people, but she preferred them one at a time. In big crowds, her throat went dry as a dust dolly and even when she *could* think of something to say, she couldn't push a single word past her paralyzed tongue. In Kansas, she had let her newspaper editorials and Papa's revolver speak for her. Out here in Oregon she felt tongue-tied. A flatland country weed in a citified rose garden.

The line of faces turned toward her, waiting. In the glow of the huge gaslight chandelier overhead they looked like a row of smiling hard-boiled eggs.

"Thank heavens you're finally heah," a voice hissed in her ear. "They cain't staht the reception until all three of us go through the receivin' line together." Fleurette stepped to the head of their little procession and signaled for Carrie to follow.

The young schoolteacher looked sweet in a high-necked mint-green dotted muslin with no trimming other than covered buttons to the hem of a softly pleated skirt. Fleurette's frothy puff-sleeved concoction of yellow taffeta engulfed her slim figure in layers of ruffles and frills, swirled into a train at the back, punctuated with a large silk rosette.

"Are we-all ready?"

"Leora, you look just lovely," Carrie whispered as Fleurette's hand reached out to snag the young schoolteacher's sleeve. "But..." Carrie paused as Fleurette pulled her into position. "Somehow you seem...shorter."

"I changed my shoes." Unable to trust her voice further, Lolly brought up the rear in silence, her lips twitching into a smile. What a picture they must make: The Three Musketeers turned out in full battle regalia.

She knew she must look like a gypsy, and she'd removed her shoes because they pinched her toes like an iron vise. But at the moment she couldn't let herself think about it.

A hand reached out, clasped hers and pumped it up and down. The next thing she knew she was being introduced to the mayor, Cyrus Bowman.

Then the mayor's imperious-looking wife, Hortense, and the banker and his wife and, next to her, his mother-in-law, all named something that sounded like Shumaker. Next came the head of the school board; the town doctor and his twin daughters; a mill owner named Hickmeyer; the newspaper editor, Orven Tillotsen; a retired railroad builder; and more wives and daughters and mothers-in-law than any one town deserved. The blur of names and faces made Lolly's head ache.

Another outstretched hand grasped hers just as Carrie, one step ahead of her, made a little moaning sound. "There he is," she murmured. "At the very end of the line."

Lolly could see nothing beyond Carrie except great clouds of yellow taffeta, but over the next mumbled introduction, Fleurette's voice rang out.

"Why, Colonel Macready, Ah have heard so much about you. So charmin' to meet you at last. Ah, too, am a Southerner."

Carrie turned her head toward Lolly and rolled her eyes before stepping up to the next person in line. "Mrs. Whipple, may I present Miss Leora Mayfield?"

Lolly tried to smile. "Mrs. Whipple."

The old woman in plum sateen shot her a keen look and nodded brusquely. "My dear."

At her side, Carrie heaved another sigh, and Lolly heard her quavery voice. "Good evening, C-Colonel."

After Carrie, Lolly was next in line. Great balls of brimstone, she was but one step away from the moment she had agonized about ever since she left Kansas—meeting a perfect stranger who would marry her.

Kellen watched the three guests of honor unknot themselves from the circle they had formed and step up to the Meet and Greet Trail, as he termed it. Barbarous custom, receiving lines. An uncivilized way to trot out the goods for inspection before the fair.

He knew Careen Gundersen from many previous occasions over the years, mostly birthday parties her parents had hosted. Careen had turned out to be a very capable young woman. Prim, maybe. And a tad...flat, somehow. The girl had always had a sensible head on her shoulders; it was beyond his understanding why on earth she, of all people, would want to enter this matrimonial charade.

Gliding down the line ahead of Careen was a meticulously groomed lady in a voluminous flounced skirt that was wound up in the back like a beehive. Quite a lot of baggage resting on that derriere. He watched her navigate from Sol Stanton to Mrs. Whipple and on toward him, her posture so rigid that her golden-blond corkscrew curls didn't bob but hung stiffly in place, even when she tossed her head. Sugar water and rag rollers, he guessed. Females put up with the damnedest things.

The women looked somewhat like curious birds, though of different species. Careen resembled a baby wren, her folded wings yet untried. The lady with the curls reminded him of a yellow silk peacock.

His gaze drifted beyond the peacock to the next person in the line, but he couldn't get a clear view of her. All he could see was the gracefully flared black skirt she wore, which, now that he studied it over the bare shoulder of Miss—what was peacock's name again?—struck him with its simplicity. Not a wren. Not a peacock, then. An elegant black swan.

"Why, Colonel Macready…" The peacock's voice chirped on. "…am a Southerner."

Kellen tore his gaze from the woman in black and focused on the beaming heart-shaped face before him. "I beg your pardon?"

"Ah said Ah am also a Southerner, like yourself."

"Actually, after nearly fifteen years in Maple Falls, I now consider myself an Oregonian."

"Oh, now, Colonel. Ah don't believe that for one li'l minute."

He made polite noises while she gushed on until he saw an opportunity to pass her on to the refreshment table, where Ruth Underwood and her husband were pouring champagne.

And applejack, he remembered from his earlier conversation with the hotel bartender. He licked his lips. He couldn't get there soon enough.

Then Careen stood before him, sighing like a spring wind through the aspen grove.

"Careen, it's nice to see you."

"Good evening, C-Colonel. I've been looking forward to this for weeks and weeks."

"As have I," he lied. "It's a bit like one of your birthday parties, isn't it? Except for the champagne, of course."

And the applejack.

"Oh, Colonel, you will dance with me later?"

"Why, of course. I've danced with you at every party since you were five years old. Remember how you used to stand on my shoe tops?"

Why was she looking at him like that?

"I remember," Careen murmured.

But Kellen was no longer listening. He found himself watching the woman in black, now speaking to old Mrs. Whipple.

Her chin tipped forward, allowing a waterfall of loose, dark curls to tumble over her bare shoulders. And God in heaven, what shoulders! Some kind of rich-looking lace festooned them, allowing glimpses of creamy flesh through the open cutwork. He tried not to stare. The way her body curved in and out made his neck burn.

She held on to Mrs. Whipple's hand for an extra-long minute, and then Careen reached out and drew her away, toward him. The woman lifted her head, and her thick, dark hair danced against those satiny shoulders.

And then she did something so completely unexpected he wondered if he was dreaming. She shut her eyes tight and stretched out her hand toward him.

"Miss Leora Mayfield," Mrs. Whipple intoned.

"Please, *please,*" she whispered. "Hold on to my hand. I am having a nervous reaction."

Kellen clasped her hand in both of his and peered into her face. The woman was attractive. Extraordinarily attractive. He studied her wide mouth, the dark lashes against her cheeks. *My God, she's beautiful.*

"Reaction to what?" he managed.

"To…this. All of these people." Her lids opened and her eyes locked with his. They were so blue and clear they made his throat ache.

"Crowds terrify me."

"Your nervous reaction is not to me, then?"

She shook her head. "Oh, no. At least not yet."

Relief coursed through him, followed by a gut-tightening unease. *Not yet?*

Kellen stood motionless, steadying her trembling hand in his. The receiving line broke up, reforming in twos and threes at the refreshment table to his right.

"I was about to have a glass of something to drink," he said gently.

"Oh, thank heaven. Could you possibly bring me one, as well? I'm so glad this is over, I feel like celebrating."

He laughed without thinking. His opinion exactly.

"But it is not over. It has just begun."

"For me it's over. The hard part, anyway. The rest is up to the Ladies Helpful Society."

Kellen winced. At this moment he didn't want to be reminded of the corner Dora Mae Landsfelter and her cadre of Helpful Ladies had backed him into. All he wanted to do was enjoy this moment for as long as he could.

"Come." He turned her toward the refreshment table. "I think we'll both need a drink before this evening is over."

Chapter Four

At the refreshment table, Kellen watched Ruth Underwood pour fizzing champagne into two glasses while her husband glugged dark gold applejack from a ceramic jug into teacups. He reached for a glass of the champagne for Miss Mayfield. Miss Mayfield, however, lifted a brimming cup of the applejack and brought it to her lips.

He kept his eyebrows from rising by sheer force of will. "You ever taste applejack before?"

She looked at him over the rim of the cup. "Never."

"Would you care to sit down first?"

"Most definitely. As soon as I drink some of this." She downed a big swallow, and he watched her eyes widen and then tear up. He lifted the cup from her fingers and steered her to the green velvet settee against the wall.

She sat down. Then jumped up. Sat down once more and bent forward as if to inspect the hem of her skirt. When she raised her head, Kellen presented the glass of champagne. She reached instead for the cup of applejack in his other hand.

A single-minded swan. "It's pretty potent," he cautioned. "More than ninety proof the way Josh Bodwin makes it."

"Good," she said. She took another swallow. "You're quite right—lots of proof." Her voice sounded raspy. Kellen drank half the glass of champagne while she gulped another mouthful of the brandy.

"Do you do this often?" he inquired. The only woman he'd ever known who could put away liquor like this was Great-Aunt Henrietta, and she'd had years of practice.

"No, I have never taken spirits before. It tastes rather like—" she thought for a moment "—crushed oak leaves."

He couldn't let her swill down any more; she'd fizzle out like a spent match. He had to think of something to distract her.

"Would you care to dance?"

Lolly looked up at him. She would give the

moon to dance with this man, tall and elegant in his black dress coat and knotted silk tie. He moved without making a single extra motion, like a mountain cat. A panther, that was it. And his eyes were positively hypnotic, an odd gray-green, and twinkly, as if he were amused at something.

"I'm afraid I can't."

"Can't?" His dark brows arched upward for a split second. "As in, you don't know how? Or you are already spoken for? Or...you don't wish to?"

"Oh, I do wish to, but..." No, she couldn't possibly tell him the truth. He would think her a complete ninny.

Or would he?

"The truth is," she heard her voice say, "I cannot raise my arms that high. My...that is, the top half of me will come undone."

Colonel Macready stared at her. Completely unnerved by her admission, Lolly fiddled with the loose knot at her bosom. He swept his gaze over the gauzy lace covering her chest and shoulders, and suddenly his face changed.

"Your trunk went on to the next stop! Is that it?"

"How on earth would you know that?"

"Happens all the time. The Russell Steam Engine Line prides itself on two-minute station stops. They'll bring it back tomorrow afternoon."

"I am relieved to hear that. In the meantime…" She sent a surreptitious glance down her front.

"In the meantime, you could waltz without raising your arms. I will simply lower mine."

She took another gulp of the interesting-tasting cider and rose unsteadily. "Very well. If you will promise not to laugh if, well, if shomeshing…that is, something…untoward occurs."

Kellen swung her away to the band's raucous rendition of "The Blue Bell of Scotland." Not a waltz, but he didn't care. He just wanted to put his arms around her and keep her talking.

They danced in silence for half a chorus, and then his black swan opened her mouth. What came out shocked him into a complete standstill.

"Colonel Macready, do you really, truly want to get married?"

He tightened his hand at her waist. She felt warm and soft under his fingers. No corset. Interesting.

"You want an honest answer, I assume?"

"Honest? Why, of course I want an honest answer. It is an honest question."

"Well, then, yes." He swallowed hard. "I do want to marry."

"But why?"

"Why! What kind of question is that? Most men want to marry at some time or other."

"Yes, but…I mean, why *this* way, with the Ladies Helpful Society stirring the pot?"

"Ah. The truth again, I gather?"

"Yes, please. It's usually much more interesting than anything one could make up."

"Well…" His throat threatened to close up tight. He swallowed again. "That is, I am comfortably situated and, well, I am getting older. And I find that I am…"

"Yes?"

He was beginning to sweat under his starched shirt. "In want of a companion. That is, a wife."

She cocked her head and the fine dark eyebrows rose. "What for? You do your own cooking, I understand. Even your own ironing." She looked from his chin to his toes and back. "And you look extremely well cared for, right down to your shiny gold cuff links."

"Miss Mayfield, let me make something clear. I do not want a wife for the purpose of caring for me. I…well, I— My God, are you always so inquisitive?"

"Yes. Always. Up until a week ago I ran a newspaper office, you see. I got quite in the habit of asking questions. Also, it must be obvious that I have a personal interest in your reasons."

"Ah, the Ladies Helpful Society again."

"Exactly. Why ever would you put three elderly ladies in charge of choosing your life's companion?"

"I can't answer that. I just plain don't know, unless maybe it's because I gave my heart away twenty years ago and at my age I don't expect to fall in love again."

"Certainly not," she said in a crisp voice. "Love is for the young."

He missed a step.

"How old are you, Miss Mayfield?"

Lolly missed a step. Her stocking-clad foot smacked into the hard toe of his left shoe. She bit her lip. "I am twenty-nine and eleven-twelfths."

"I am forty-three…"

She gazed up at his chin. My goodness, he didn't look a day over thirty-five, except for that streak of silver at his temple. And the faint whisker shadow visible on his chin; why, he looked rugged and manly and…even a little dangerous.

"And two-thirds." A conspiratorial glint of humor showed in his eyes.

"Ow!" She collided with his foot again.

"Miss Mayfield?"

"Colonel Macready?"

"Leora, is it?"

"Lolly."

"My given name is Kellen. My grandmother's family name. And…" He stopped in the middle of the ballroom and stood looking down into her face. "I would like—"

"Oh, theah you are, Colonel! Ah've requested a Virginia reel. You will partner me, won't you?"

Fleurette eyed Lolly with a look that reminded her of a green glass bottle on her mother's medicine shelf. The one that contained castor oil.

"That is, when y'all are finished heah, of course."

Lolly caught Colonel Macready's eye. Some devilish imp inside her pushed her lips open. "I do believe the colonel is quite finished."

She spun away and limped—unobtrusively, she hoped—back to the green velvet settee where she sank down onto the soft cushion with a sigh. She would never, never learn to keep her mouth shut.

She bit her lip and watched the colonel swing Fleurette up and down the line of dancers while the band boomed out a reel. Fleurette's yellow silk train twitched and jumped with a life of its own while the shiny brass instruments and one violin warbled on.

Lolly kept time with her stockinged toes hidden under her skirt, sipping the cup of apple cider she'd left on the side table. It tasted different now. Better. Warm and soothing when it reached her stomach. Her chest began to feel floaty, as if any moment it might sail away from the rest of her body.

Not only that, she thought in alarm, the tips of her— *Heavens, she shouldn't be having such thoughts!*

Her nipples swelled into hardened peaks anyway. "Stop that!" she ordered under her breath.

She focused her attention on the yellow swirl of silk taffeta in the colonel's arms and then on the colonel himself. How graceful his motions were as he swooped his partner around the room. And how tall and straight he was. She'd seen tall, handsome men before, but she had never seen one like this.

His tousled dark hair and mustache gave him a slightly rakish air, even though he was correctly dressed right up to his chin. His mouth moved, saying something to Fleurette, and his teeth flashed in a grin. Then his lips closed, leaving just a hint of a smile.

Fleurette gazed up into his face, her laughter trilling over the sound of the fiddle. Over the cornet, as well. The colonel's chiseled features remained impassive, but his eyes—those unsettling eyes—

like liquid jade—flicked over the line of dancers as if looking for something and then returned to his partner.

Fleurette's lashes beat like gold butterfly wings against her pinkened cheeks. The colonel tightened his lips and looked up at the chandelier.

Lolly sat upright. *At the chandelier?* Was he bored? With the most ladified lady in the entire room? Why, they looked simply wonderful dancing together. The perfect couple.

So why was he staring at the ceiling?

Lolly's toes curled under. A man as heart-stoppingly handsome as he was would always want a pretty partner on his arm. A pretty wife.

A pretty, *slim* wife.

Her breath gusted out in a rush. Oh, bother. She was not going to cry. Not one drop. She most certainly was not.

She would avert her eyes and…and have another sip of cider. She drew the cup to her lips.

Empty? Over the rim she saw Colonel Macready bow over Fleurette's daintily extended hand, gently disengage himself from her fingers and head in Lolly's direction.

Her heart flip-flopped. Her belly felt cold, and then hot, and then cold again. And farther down, between her thighs, a secret part of her throbbed to life.

"Oh, not you, too," she breathed.

Before the colonel had completed three of his long-legged strides, a spoon tinked against a glass and everything—noise, motion and Kellen Macready—came to a halt.

"Ladies and gentlemen, may I have your attention?" Lolly tensed at Dora Mae Landsfelter's commanding voice. Something momentous was going to happen. She could feel it.

"The Ladies Helpful Society of Maple Falls has a wonderful surprise for you this evening. A most unusual surprise, but I am assured by the committee members, Minnie Sullivan and Ruth Underwood, that it is perfectly proper. Colonel Macready? Will you step forward?"

"A Question Bee!" Carrie stared at Dora Mae Landsfelter's beaming face, then tipped her head toward Lolly. "Does she mean like a Spelling Bee?" she intoned.

"I suppose so," Lolly whispered back. "Why should our knowledge of those things matter to him? He wants a wife, not an encyclopedia."

"Well," Carrie ventured, "his wife will also be

the mother of his children. Wouldn't he want her to be educated?''

Fleurette swept toward them, a swirl of bobbing yellow ruffles. ''What are y'all whisperin' about? Are y'all talkin' about me?''

''Not you at all,'' Carrie assured her. ''About the Question Bee.''

''Oh, that.'' Fleurette tossed her curls. ''Ah 'spect the colonel...'' Her green eyes swept the room. ''My, he *is* handsome, isn't he? Ah think he desires knowledge of our background and upbringing.''

''He knows everything about me,'' Carrie wailed. ''What will I say?''

''Just tell him the borin' ol' truth, honey.'' Fleurette bent toward the two women. ''Could Ah join y'all on that settee? Mah poor feet ache somethin' awful after all that dancin'.''

Carrie and Lolly shifted apart to make room, and Fleurette wedged her derriere between them. Two large puffs of yellow silk ballooned out on each side, spilling over Carrie's green dress and Lolly's black skirt.

''Oh, my, that *does* feel so much better. Now, what were we—''

''Ladies and gentlemen?'' A spoon tinked for attention and the three gray-haired Helpful Ladies gathered in front of the refreshment table. Minnie Sullivan's hands darted and swooped before her bosom. "Let me tell, Dora Mae. I was the one who thought of it."

"It was my idea, Min. Don't you remember? You had just finished your second serving of Ruth's applesauce cake and—"

"Why, Dora Mae Landsfelter, don't tell me you counted my desserts?"

"Goddammit to hell," a deep voice rolled over the assembly. "I cannot abide squabbling females."

"Oh, of course not, Colonel," the two women sang in unison.

Colonel Macready strode through the tittering crowd. "It was *my* idea, if I remember correctly. I proposed it to Mrs. Underwood an hour ago."

Minnie's hands fluttered. "Oh, yes. Yes, you are quite right."

"And since it is the only suggestion the Helpful Ladies have allowed me to contribute—" he made his way to the front of the room "—let's get on with it."

"Well put, Kelly," a voice said.

"Ask yer questions, Colonel," another man added. "We're sure 'nuf curious about what these here ladies think about…things."

Beside her, Lolly felt Fleurette's silk-swathed body stiffen. Could the woman be nervous? She had sufficient fancy background and aristocratic upbringing to answer a hundred of the colonel's questions. Lolly could only pray none of them would touch on Abolitionist newspapers in Kansas.

"Question One," Dora Mae Landsfelter announced. "Colonel? You may do the honors."

Kellen stood perfectly still, surveying the three samples of femininity squashed together, their fluffed-out feathers settling over their nests. The peacock's showy plumage nearly buried both Careen and Miss Mayfield.

He chuckled under his breath. Life was too short not to enjoy this. He sank into an upholstered wing-backed chair, loosened his neckpiece and picked up his cue from Dora Mae.

"Question One," he reiterated. "What about Maple Falls interests you the most? Miss Gundersen?"

Careen jerked as if an elbow had been jabbed into her ribs. "My students," she said without hesitation. "They ask so many questions. Naturally, I try to answer every one."

A murmur of approval ran around the room. It sounded curiously like industrious bees humming in a hive. Kellen leaned back against the brocade and smiled at Careen. She was very practical-minded, the epitome of a dedicated schoolteacher.

"Miss LeClair?"

Fleurette tilted her head coquettishly. Two bright eyes fixed on him and then disappeared under a fluttery fringe of descending amber eyelashes. The perfect rosebud mouth opened.

"Why, Colonel, what interests me most here in Maple Falls is your home."

Someone—it sounded like Sol Stanton—guffawed, but Miss LeClair proceeded undaunted. "After all, a bride wants to know wheah she will be livin'."

Kellen kept his expression as impassive as he could. A shot of applejack would help, but Matt Underwood was whispering in his wife's ear and Kellen couldn't catch his eye. He turned his attention to the black swan.

"Miss Mayfield?"

She did look lovely in that lacy black getup, her cheeks rosy, her blue eyes slightly unfocused and her nose...

Good God, her nose was bright red! She was snockered! An English heritage, he would guess; their cheeks and noses reddened under the influence of spirits.

He wanted to laugh. Correction, he wanted to

throttle her. Something inside him couldn't bear to watch her make a fool of herself. In the next second he wanted to protect her. Oh, hell, he wanted to...

It was too late to retract the question. *Say something simple,* he urged her. *Something short, using words of only one syllable.*

The tip of her tongue slipped out to wet her lips and he heard a tiny sound. Oh, Lord, she had the hiccups.

Her mouth opened. "I think..." She closed her lips and frowned, and Kellen saw her throat tighten in another spasm.

"I think what interests me most about Ma-aple Falls is you, Colonel."

Kellen blinked. "Me!"

"Precise-ly. What I find most intri-guing is why you would let the La-dies Helpful Society choose a wife for you. Oh, I understand about building the new sch-ool, but, to be honesht, uh honest, I would think—"

Kellen sent a desperate look toward the refreshment table. *Do something!*

Dora Mae nodded. "Question Two," she stated in a piercing tone.

Thank God. Kellen wet his own lips and dug his notes out of his breast pocket. "Yes, well. Question

Two is...what makes you happy? Miss Gundersen?''

Careen's face lit up. "Oh, that's easy, Colonel. I like solving things, like riddles. Or arithmetic problems. I like to figure things out."

Another approving buzz circled around the hive.

"Miss LeClair?"

The pale eyelashes swooped down, then up. "Ah am happy when Ah can please others. Especially one particular Other, if you take my meanin'."

Kellen unclenched his fingers. Meaning taken, yes. But believed? Not unless pigs flew south in the winter.

"Miss..." He caught himself just in time. Had the black swan had time to conquer her hiccups? He bent forward on the pretext of flicking a speck off his trouser leg and sent a surreptitious glance at Miss Mayfield.

She sat straight as a queen, her hands clasped in her lap—or what he could see of her lap under Miss Peacock's voluminous skirt. And she was looking him straight in the eye. A challenge.

Ask me, her expression said. *Get it over with.*

"Miss Mayfield?"

"Flowers," she blurted. "Flowers make me happy. Yellow ones. And sunsets and bread-baking smells and peach ice cream and running barefoot

in long green grass and lovingsomeonelike-
Ilovedmyfather...." She paused for air. "There's
much more, but that's all I can think of at the moment."

So there, her gaze said.

Well-done. He congratulated her with a silent
nod.

And just in time, too. Miss Mayfield's eyelids
were beginning to droop. The applejack had caught
up with her.

"And now," Dora Mae announced with a flour-
ish, "the Last Question. Colonel?"

Kellen crumpled his notes in his fist and took a
deep breath. The question he really wanted to ask
wasn't on his list. In fact he hadn't thought of it
until this moment.

He shouldn't inquire about something so personal. But he had to know. He *had* to.

He took in a deep lungful of air and plunged.
"The last question is, Why on earth are you interested in marrying me?"

All three women gaped at him.

Careen recovered first. "Every eligible female in
this town would simply die to marry you, Colonel.
Surely you don't find that surprising?"

Miss LeClair responded as Kellen would have
predicted. "Ah have heard on good authority that

yoah a brave military officer and a Southern gentlemen. And that is exactly what Ah am lookin'
for.''

And his swan?

Miss Mayfield's head nodded toward the yellow-
silk-clad shoulder on her right.

"Miss Mayfield?" He sent her an urgent unspoken message. *Wake up.* Hoping the sound of his
voice would rouse her, he repeated the question in
a louder tone. "Why are you interested in marrying
me?"

The blue eyes popped open. "Why? My gracious, I think that would be obvious. I don't want
to be an old maid!"

Laughter. Then the humming of animated conversation rose and eddied about the room; it
sounded exactly like a hive of bees beginning to
swarm. Kellen was too stunned to respond.

Squeezed between the settee arm and Fleurette's
voluminous skirts, Lolly decided she had to stand
up. Either that or fall asleep right where she sat.
Already her toes were numb and the tingly feeling
was beginning to move up her calves toward her
knees.

She tried to rise, but she couldn't struggle past
the enveloping mountain of yellow silk. "Ahem,"
she murmured.

Fleurette chattered away without dropping a beat.

Lolly shifted her weight. "Excuse me," she murmured. She tried to press down the puffs of skirt material.

No reaction. Fleurette's voice drawled on. And on.

Lolly didn't want to make a scene, but she had to get out of there. *Now.* She could feel the lace shawl pulling away from the top of her camisole; two more minutes and it would unwind completely and she would be sitting here in nothing but her camisole!

Clasping one hand to her bosom to hold things together, she poked the other under the yellow silk, aimed for solid flesh and pinched.

"Oo-ooooh!" Fleurette sprang to her feet. "Well, really," she huffed. "Ah do declare..." Her voice trailed off when the colonel stepped forward.

"Is something wrong?"

Lolly flinched. Had he seen what she did?

"N-no," Fleurette stammered. She sent Lolly a venomous look. "Ah guess Ah was mistaken."

But from the glint of amusement in the colonel's eyes, Lolly would wager he knew very well what she'd done.

Now that she was unencumbered, she would try again to stand up and make as polite an exit as she could manage, considering that her head felt light and kind of swirly. She would rock her weight forward and straighten to a standing position, despite her dizziness.

She commanded her knees to flex. Nothing happened.

She stiffened her spine. On the count of three, then.

"Leora?" Carrie peered at her from the other end of the green settee.

"One," Lolly said.

"One what? Are you all right? You look…"

"Two," Lolly muttered under her breath.

"Leora?" A hand stretched toward her.

Three.

She tried. She really tried. But ever so slowly, she began to tip sideways. *Oh, mercy and botherment.* Her cheek touched the velvet. My, it felt so good to close her eyes and…

The next thing she knew, someone—a man she guessed from his strength and his piney-musky scent—was lifting her upright. She opened her eyes to see Kellen Macready's face much closer to hers than seemed proper.

"Oh, h'lo," she murmured. "You smell good."

Kellen's voice vibrated against her ear. "Miss Mayfield, put your arms around my neck."

"I would if I could," she whispered. "But they have stopped working."

"In that case..." He lifted her off the settee, rolled her against his chest and began moving.

"Oh, please," she moaned. "Not sho fast. I feel like I've sprouted wings and I'll fly right up to the ceiling."

"You won't," he assured her.

"How do you know?"

This time an unmistakable laugh rumbled in his chest. "Gravity is on my side."

His voice sounded near her temple. "Close your eyes, Miss Mayfield. And don't talk."

Lolly obeyed. Oh, but it felt lovely to be held in his arms. Her head pressed against his neck; the silk tie he wore tickled her chin. He did smell good. So good she wanted to lick his skin and taste it.

"Miss Mayfield has fainted, I believe." His deep voice resonated against her ear.

Oh, no, I haven't fainted, an inner voice reminded. *I never faint. Even if I think I might die, I don't faint.* At this moment she might be floating with the angels near the ceiling, but she certainly had not lost reason or consciousness.

Voices ebbed and sighed around her. One in particular cut through the woolly-bear feeling in her brain. "Well, Ah never..."

A door banged open and a rush of cooler air blew against her face and shoulders. As he descended the stairs, the colonel's body sent a little jolt into hers at every step. She counted all eighteen.

"Miss Mayfield, where is your room?"

The sweet, drowsy feeling was spreading through her limbs. It was so delicious she didn't want it to end. She shook her head.

He groaned. "You can talk now."

"Dowanna," she mumbled. "Wanna stay right here."

He made the funny noise inside his chest and then groaned again. "You can't."

"Why not?"

"For one thing, it would cause talk."

"Don't care. Been there before."

A short silence. "For another, it would upset Dora Mae Landsfelter and the Ladies Helpful Society."

Her lids flew open. "Oh! I forgot all about Dora Mae and...that. Tha's why I was so scared all evening. Tha's why I came to Maple Falls in th' first plash. Place."

"What is your room number?" he asked again.

"Ish room number..." Her mind went blank.

Kellen waited, breathing less steadily. "Yes?"

"Jush look for my shoes. I left them jush inside the door. Have pointy toes and they pinch."

He guessed he had no choice. He stepped along the hallway with his burden in his arms, testing doorknobs, until he found one that opened. Sure enough, a pair of black leather pumps leaned against the baseboard. He kicked the door shut behind him, walked to the bed and laid her on top of the quilt. She curled up like a kitten, folded her hands under her chin and was asleep in an instant.

Kellen's chest did something funny, as if a ripple had zigzagged from his throat to his belly. What the devil?

He spent a good five minutes just staring at her, noticing the scattering of freckles across her nose, the loose dark hair, sneaking from the bun at the back of her neck, the faint laugh lines in the outer corners of her eyes. She sure looked different from Careen and The Peacock.

And she sure felt different when he held her.

Damn. He had to get out of here. Now. Either that or risk a scandal that would destroy Miss Mayfield's reputation.

He'd send Careen down to check on her. And tomorrow...

Oh, God, the Helpful Ladies and their bride competition! Tomorrow it would all start in earnest. How adept could a newspaper editor from dry, windswept Kansas be at greensward croquet?

Chapter Five

Shielding her eyes from the bright sunlight, Lolly moved along the board sidewalk keeping each footstep as smooth as possible to avoid jarring her head. This morning, the mere tap of her shoes on the wood planks sounded like cannon fire.

There it was. Bodwin's Mercantile. She pushed open the door and bypassed a bushel basket of apples perched on top of a pickle barrel. The thought of food, even a tiny bite of apple, sent her stomach into rebellion.

"Something I can do for you, miss?" The lanky man behind the counter wiped his hands on his denim apron and leaned toward her. He had a breakfasty smell about him, as if he had a grilled sausage in his pocket.

Lolly gulped. "Yes, I—"

"Got just about everything in stock 'cept skunk traps and silver-tipped walking sticks."

"Do you carry ladies' outerwear?"

He surveyed her with penetrating blue eyes. "New in town, aren'tcha?"

Lolly swallowed. "Why do you say that?"

"Well, now, ma'am. Anybody's lived here more'n twenty-four hours knows Dora Mae Landsfelter."

"Yes, I am acquainted with Mrs. Landsfelter."

"Well, then, you know why we don't carry ladies' outerwear. Or un-outerwear, neither."

"I'm afraid I don't follow," Lolly said. "What has your mercantile stock to do with Mrs. Landsfelter?" She sensed a story here, maybe an amusing one, if she could worm it out of the shopkeeper. She could use a bit of levity this morning; her head buzzed as if it were crammed full of angry grasshoppers.

The lean man chuckled. "Name's Joshua Bodwin, ma'am. Pleased to make your acquaintance."

"Leora Mayfield."

"Oh, yes. You're one of the brides. I recognize you from the reception last night."

"You do?" She desperately hoped it was the first part of the evening, and not the last, which she had spent dangling from the arms of Colonel Macready.

"Yep. Kellen Macready pointed you out."

"He did? What did he s-say?" Lolly's voice cracked.

Mr. Bodwin grinned. "That you were partial to my applejack. I make it myself, don'tcha know. And deliver it to the hotel for their fancy do's. I was hopin' 'tweren't too potent for womenfolk."

"Oh, no," Lolly fibbed. "It tasted quite wonderful. So…relaxing for a social gathering."

"Why, thank you, ma'am. Now, about Dora Mae Landsfelter and outerwear. It's like this. One of her growed-up sons lost all his money breeding camels for the army, which decided in the end they didn't want 'em."

"I don't see what--"

"But young Garth, he married himself a gal, Hulda Jane, that's a whiz with a needle, so Miz Landsfelter set her up in business sewin' ladies' duds. Landsfelter Ladieswear, two doors down past the sheriff's office. She can whip up most anything overnight."

Lolly bit her lip. Overnight wasn't soon enough. "The trouble of it is, Mr. Bodwin, my trunk, containing my entire wardrobe, won't be here until noon today, and the Helpful Ladies are holding

some sort of sporting event at ten o'clock this
morning.''

"That'd be the croquet match, Miss Mayfield.
All the ladies of Maple Falls are plumb taken with
the game.''

Lolly's kindling hope sputtered out like a doused
match. "Croquet? That's a skill I've never ac-
quired.''

"Come to the right place to learn,'' Mr. Bodwin
said. "I musta sold eight or ten croquet sets just
this past month. Everybody in town thinks he, or
she, is an expert.''

Except for her. Lolly had never had time to pick
up such social skills; every spare minute she had
was spent writing articles and setting type.

"Mr. Bodwin, I do not need the help of Mrs.
Landsfelter's daughter-in-law. I need *your* help
now on a different matter.''

The storekeeper's eyes widened with interest.
"What kinda help?''

"The only garment I have at the moment is the
travel suit I'm wearing. But the jacket is too heavy
and uncomfortable to wear for sports, so I need
something lighter. Looser. Something like a—''

The storekeeper snapped his long fingers. "Got
just the thing, miss. Course it'll look a mite odd,
but...'' He whisked out from behind the counter

and disappeared into an aisle formed by two towering shelves facing each other.

"Here." He thrust a man's red plaid shirt at her. "Biggest size I carry, so should be plenty roomy for your…" The man blushed crimson. "Uh, why don't you try it on?" He ushered her through a curtain and ducked back into his store.

The garment did have plenty of room for her bosom. However, the shoulder seams drooped halfway down her biceps, and the cuffs hung past her fingers. Still, she could button it all the way to her chin and it didn't gape open where her breasts pressed against the fabric. She could raise both arms and bend at the waist.

"Bless you, Mr. Bodwin," she murmured. She could fold the sleeves back and tuck the long tail into the waistband of her black faille skirt. If wearing a man's shirt didn't scandalize the townspeople, she would be another step closer to her goal of escaping the prison of spinsterhood.

Joshua Bodwin accepted her money, wrapped the shirt up in brown paper and tied the parcel with twine, then leaned over the counter toward her. "You know anything about playin' croquet, Miss Mayfield?"

"Not one single thing," she confessed. A hot, panicky feeling roiled in her belly.

His weathered face took on a look of concern. "Not much I can show you in half an hour, but let me tell you something important 'bout the strategy of the game."

"S-strategy? I thought you just hit a wooden ball of some sort."

He glanced at a customer who just entered the store, and lowered his voice. "Keep your ball out of the line of fire."

Lolly had no idea what that meant, but she nodded anyway. "Line of fire," she repeated with a nod. "I'll remember."

The customer kept his back to them, studying the display of kerosene lamps hanging from a rafter.

Mr. Bodwin bent closer. "Don't seem sportin' to have the whole town cheerin' for Miss Careen and nobody pullin' for you. So…" His bright-eyed gaze flicked to the man at the lantern display and back.

"So *I'm* gonna root for you." He handed her the wrapped package and patted her hand. "Always did have a soft spot for the underdog."

"Underdog? There is one other player besides myself who is a stranger in town. Miss LeClair. Would you root for her, too?"

Joshua Bodwin rolled his eyes toward the ceiling. "I heard tell that Miss LeClair was the Loosiana State Ladies Croquet Champion last summer. And Miss Careen, why, she's been playing croquet since she could walk. That's why I'm rootin' for *you*."

Now she understood. Lolly the Underdog. Not only had she never before laid her hand on a croquet bat—they did play the game with bats, didn't they?—she would once again be oddly dressed in something she'd improvised at the very last minute. Oh, Papa, you were right: You can't cross a chasm in two small steps. To cross *this* chasm, she'd have to fly!

"Mr. Bodwin," she whispered so the other customer couldn't overhear. "I would also like to purchase a straw hat, please. With the widest brim you can find."

"All I got is men's hats, mostly for fieldwork."

"Do you think such a hat would keep the sun out of my eyes?"

"Yes, miss," he said in a puzzled tone. "Guess so."

"Then it will do admirably. And have you a leather belt? One that would fit me? I cannot march into battle with half my armor missing."

Despite the doubtful look the shopkeeper sent her, he found the named items and wrapped them up, as well. As quickly and quietly as she could, she gathered up her purchases and slipped out the front door.

As soon as the bell over the entrance stopped jangling, Kellen Macready moved away from the lantern display and stepped to the counter. "Josh."

"Kelly. Thought that was you. Didn't want to say anything till Miss Mayfield left. Thought she'd prob'ly not want to be distracted by anything, seeing as how she don't know beans 'r barleycorn about this croquet clambake Dora Mae's planning."

"You going to referee the match?"

"No one asked me to."

"I'm asking. I want it to be fair."

Joshua snickered. "Not a chance in hell, Kelly. Miss Mayfield's never played before. It's David against *two* Goliaths."

"I was afraid of that. Dora Mae assumes everybody does what *she* does. In this case, play nine-wicket croquet.

"Worse," Joshua said, pursing his lips. "*Oregon* croquet. Ain't like the other versions. Kell, how'd you let Dora Mae railroad you into this fandango, anyway?"

Kellen sighed. "I turned my brain off for sixty seconds, and she nailed me."

"Can't you get un-nailed? Miss Mayfield seems like a nice lady. She even liked my applejack. I'd hate to see her get humiliated."

"I gave Dora Mae my word, Josh.

"Damn fool."

Kellen winced inwardly. He hated to see any woman hurt, but especially one like Leora Mayfield. She was a fish about as far from a pond as she could get.

"Just keep it on the level, Josh. Maybe Miss Mayfield will surprise us."

With the hangover she must have from last night's applejack, she'd be feeling pretty rocky. He wondered how she'd gotten out of bed this morning without someone pouring a gallon of black coffee down her throat.

"Match starts at ten. They're setting up the court now on my back lawn." He exited the mercantile, heard Josh lock the door behind him. A Closed sign popped into the front window.

Kellen laughed softly. He guessed he wasn't the only one anxious to see how the morning turned out. "Miss Mayfield!"

Footsteps clumped down the boardwalk behind Lolly. She couldn't look. It would be someone, a man she knew by the voice, she had met at the reception last night. No matter who it was she couldn't face him. Firstly, she wouldn't remember his name. Secondly, he, and no doubt his wife or his daughter or sister or mother, had witnessed her first—and last, she resolved—acquaintanceship with hard spirits.

She picked up her pace.

"Miss Mayfield! Leora."

Oh! Lolly stopped dead. It was *him*. Colonel Macready. She could tell by the way he pronounced her name, sliding off the *r* with a slight Southern lilt.

"Colonel Macready." With the morning sun at his back, the gray streaks at his dark temples shone like silver. His gray-green eyes surveyed her with what she'd swear was amusement.

"Well?" she said, louder than she intended.

He gave a soft laugh. "Yes, are you?"

"Am I what? Oh, am I well?" What she was this morning was slow-witted. She opened her mouth to say, "Yes, quite well," but something entirely different came tumbling out.

"How did I get into my bed last night without a stitch of—"

"Careen," he said quickly. "I carried you from the ballroom into your room. You told me about

your shoes, remember? Then I sent Careen down
to look after you. How do you feel this morning?''

"Awful. Like there's a windmill in my head.''

"Applejack will do that, all right.''

"Is that what you call it? The stuff that tasted
like oak leaves? I don't think I—''

"No, I won't offer it again.'' He smiled when
he said it. Lolly couldn't tell if it was an amused
smile or a kindly one.

"Are you feeling up to Dora Mae's croquet
match this morning?''

"Oh, yes. Mr. Bodwin gave me some strategy
tips.''

"A more important matter is whether you can
bend over and sight down a greensward.''

"I believe I can, yes.'' She was afraid to try a
full tilt at the moment, so she did the next best
thing. She dipped down into a curtsy of sorts, just
to see how a change in elevation affected her.
When she bobbed up, her vision went swirly.
"I—''

"Here.'' A steadying hand, then two steadying
hands grasped her shoulders and held her.

And kept on holding her. She looked up to see
him grinning at her. He had white, white teeth, she
thought irrationally. And a dimple. Just one, but it

softened his sharply chiseled features just enough to make him seem boyish.

He is gorgeous, Lolly thought. *Really and truly gorgeous.* Like a statue of a king or a god. Something touched by the divine. He would be so easy to fall in love with.

Why *had* he never married?

Good gracious, what a thought! "Colonel, I must ask you something."

He turned amused eyes on her. "Ask away."

"It's not that I am nosy. Well, yes, I suppose I am, having run a newspaper for so many years. It's for my own peace of mind, you see."

"I see."

She hesitated. "Last night, when you, uh, carried me to my room, did my dress, um, did the top come undone?"

Kellen decided lying was the better part of valor in this case. The truth was the lacy black swath of fabric that covered her shoulders in the ballroom covered nothing of the kind by the time he plopped her onto her bed. She need not know the details.

"Not that I noticed."

Just as she need not know how tempted he'd been to stay and watch the rest of her covering disappear. There were times, he reminded himself, when being a gentleman was not as much fun as—

"Men lie all the time," she remarked out of the blue.

Kellen blinked. Her statement sent a guilty thrill into his midsection. Did she guess how long he'd stood there, looking down at her?

"Did you like it? My dress?"

"Very much," he said honestly.

Too damn much. What was he thinking, admiring the female attributes of *this* woman when he would probably end up married to one of the other two?

"I look forward to watching the croquet match this morning," he said. "Good day, Miss Mayfield."

With a nod, she moved off toward the hotel, and Kellen stood watching her dark skirt sway with the motion of her softly rounded hips. By the time she reached the hotel steps, his mouth was dry as a dust devil.

Cut the palaver, Kell. It's her you want to watch.

Chapter Six

Lolly stuffed the new red plaid shirt inside her waistband, looped the overlong leather belt at her waist and adjusted the oversize straw hat. She was as ready as she would ever be.

Just as she came down the red-painted steps of the hotel, she spied Carrie in a demure blue sateen and Fleurette in a froth of summery white dimity. Even her flower-bedecked garden hat sported a fluttering white ribbon. She looked as cool as a dish of vanilla ice cream.

Fleurette tipped her parasol sideways so she could study Lolly's outfit. ''Mah Lord, what *are* you traipsin' around in?''

''Actually,'' Carrie interjected, ''it looks quite… practical.''

Lolly met Fleurette's green-eyed gaze with as

much aplomb as she could muster. "It's all the rage back in Kansas. Because of the wind, you know."

"The wind? The wind makes it fashionable to wear such...such..." Fleurette floundered for words.

"Of course," Lolly said airily. "The red plaid keeps away mosquitos, and all the ladies wear hats like these." She fingered the edge of the oversize field hand's straw hat balanced on her head. "Otherwise, the hawks fly off with them in their talons."

"Hawks!"

Carrie gave Lolly's arm a little nudge and opened her mouth to speak. Instead she emitted a blurp of helpless laughter and clapped her hand over her lips. Fleurette snapped her parasol into position and strode ahead.

"How *could* you pull her leg like that?" Careen whispered.

"Easily. My trunk hasn't arrived yet, my head aches and the constantly expressed shock of that bundle of dimity fluff sets my teeth on edge!"

Carrie nodded. Without another word they followed Fleurette across the town square to Spruce Street, up four blocks and over a stone footbridge, then down a sycamore-shaded lane to the colonel's residence on Peach Street.

The ornate gray-and-white house took up most of the block, and the lush green yard surrounding the structure looked like a meticulously groomed park.

Fleurette stared admiringly through the scrolled iron gate. "Mah gracious sakes, y'all ever see so much green grass in all your life?"

Carrie pointed through the black metal. "Back there about a dozen yards the grass slopes down to the river."

"My, oh my," Fleurette breathed. "There'll be garden parties, picnics, ice cream socials, even boating events.... Why, it will be pure fun livin' here!"

Carrie blinked. "Aren't you counting your chickens a bit early?"

Fleurette tossed her perfectly coiffured curls and pushed through the gate.

"You have to marry him first," Carrie called after her. Lolly yanked her arm.

"Oh, all right, I'll be good. But honestly, Leora, doesn't she get your goat sometimes?"

Lolly bit her tongue so hard her eyes burned. All three of them might end up in Maple Falls, one way or another. Whatever happened, it would not be wise to make an enemy of a woman who might end up marrying Colonel Macready.

At least for now. She clamped one hand on her hat and trod after Carrie. She would think about Fleurette later.

The croquet court was laid out in a double-diamond pattern, the nine painted wire wickets adorning the velvety green lawn like loops of white lace.

Lolly wrinkled her nose at the sharp, clean scent of the grass under her feet. She hated to mash it down with her fancy high-heeled shoes. Even more, she hated the thought of the guests that would trample the area in Fleurette's imagined round of social events. In one season, the beautiful grounds would be ruined.

Was that what the colonel would want?

She watched the growing throng of onlookers gather around the perimeter of the playing field. The mayor and his wife, Cyrus and Hortense Bowman, the Shumaker sisters and, oh God, Mr. Tillotsen, the newspaper editor! All coming to watch her make a fool of herself. Again. She sucked in a choking breath.

Joshua Bodwin strode back and forth, shooing the crowd behind the chalked boundary lines. Even the three Ladies Helpful Society members were herded away from the playing court. Joshua appeared to take particular pleasure in ordering Dora Mae Landsfelter a respectable distance behind the line. "Ladies, keep yer skirts 'n petticoats from dustin' off my chalk lines! And you gents, watch yer boots."

The storekeeper gestured the three players forward to where a wheeled wooden cart loaded with playing equipment stood near a striped wooden peg pounded into the earth.

Lolly studied the cart. Not bats, she realized. Odd-shaped wooden mallets. How on earth did you grip them?

Fleurette floated gracefully over the ground like a fluttering butterfly, eyed the cart, gave Joshua Bodwin a wide smile and selected a mallet. Lolly watched her delicate hands close around the wooden shaft, then take a practice swing.

Fleurette swung the mallet off to one side to clear her skirt. Lolly glanced down at her own attire. She could push her gored skirt out of the way, but…

Careen gripped her mallet with her hands placed farther apart, Lolly noted. Her practice strokes were smooth and controlled.

Then Joshua motioned Lolly forward. *Please, Lord, let me look like I know what I'm doing.*

The wooden shaft felt thin and wobbly in her grasp. She bent over, lined up the mallet head parallel with her right foot, as both Careen and Fleurette had done. Even with her skirt brushed to one side, she was off balance. The mallet felt awkward in her hands and uncontrollable on the backswing.

Joshua gave her a nod and raised one arm for silence.

"Play will now begin," he bellowed.

Kellen smiled when Dora Mae and the other two Helpful Ladies posted themselves in the prime viewing area, under the shade of a towering ash tree. Croquet was Dora Mae's favorite pastime; she wouldn't want to miss a single minute of the event.

He shifted his gaze to the three competitors, clustered in a knot near the starting peg. One fluffed-out white peacock, one quiet wren with blue feathers, and one—

Good God, what had happened to his black swan?

Her head covering struck him first, a man's straw work hat with a high, rounded crown and a wide brim that dipped over her forehead and tipped rakishly up at the sides. It looked like a cross between a sombrero and a Dakota cavalry hat. Two sizes too big for her head, it rested on her ears. And to keep it on, she'd tied it under her chin with a length of grocer's twine.

His gaze moved down to her blouse. Shirt, rather. A man's, if he wasn't mistaken. Red plaid. Even with the sleeves rolled up he could see it was four sizes bigger than she was. Except, he noted, where it buttoned over her chest; that part fit just fine. She'd wrapped a wide black belt of soft deerskin around her middle, and looped the ends into a knot at her waist.

Kellen stared. Actually, she was a standout. A red-breasted blackbird peering out from under an outlandish oversize hat. He chuckled. Miss Mayfield was by far the most interesting-looking object in his backyard, and that included the refreshment table Mrs. Squires was setting up beneath the dogwood bower. He hoped his housekeeper would serve whiskey in addition to lemonade. His insides felt edgy.

He watched the toss-up for playing order. The three women's hands climbed up the mallet shaft, and he noted with amusement how Fleurette LeClair scrunched her fingers close together so she would be sure to end up on top. She claimed the blue ball and the right to play first. Careen would play second with red. His swan-pecker would be last, using the black ball.

Off to the side, young Hank Morehouse paced back and forth like an expectant father. Next to him, Sol Stanton puffed blue smoke out of his pipe. When Fleurette took her place at the starting peg, the smoke stopped suddenly and the retired railroad magnate signaled young Hank to stop moving.

A sharp *clack* and Fleurette's blue ball whizzed through the first wicket. Another stroke, another wicket and when Fleurette's turn ended, she was one shot short of gaining the third wire hoop.

'"Two points for Blue,'' Josh yelled.

Careen whacked her ball with assurance and when she approached the third wicket, she purposely aimed for Fleurette's ball, knocking it farther afield.

Kellen nodded in approval. Since the wickets had to be cleared in strict order, the white peacock would have to backtrack and reapproach the hoop her ball had bypassed.

Careen then cleared her designated wicket and, with her extra shot, she once more clacked her ball into Fleurette's blue one. Smart girl.

And then Kellen noticed something else. Leora Mayfield was studying every move the other two players made, assessing the position of each ball, surreptitiously testing her grip on her mallet. So intent was her concentration that she did not move a single muscle until Careen's turn ended.

In that instant Kellen grasped the truth. Leora had never played croquet. She was trying to learn the game in the few short minutes before her turn.

Out of the corner of his vision he spotted Sol, his face intent, his unlit pipe clenched between his teeth. Well, well. One of the three females had caught the railroad man's attention. Perhaps Miss Mayfield, from the way he shifted his stance when she stepped forward to strike off.

When the figure in the round-top hat bent over her mallet, Hank Morehouse stopped midstride. "Come on, Miss Leora! Whack it good!"

Josh Bodwin's head swiveled. "Let's have quiet before a shot!"

Leora edged up to her black ball, shifted her weight to her front foot as Careen and Fleurette had done, and drew her mallet back. She hesitated so long, Kellen wondered if she'd fallen asleep in that position.

Suddenly she straightened, stuffed her skirt between her knees, brought her mallet back between her legs and drove the shaft forward. Under the ash tree, Dora Mae Landsfelter snapped her mouth shut and began to fan herself.

The ball zipped forward, clearing two wickets.

Leora shot again using the same splay-legged stance, and this time her black ball tapped Careen's red one.

She looked to Josh. "What happens now?"

"Player gets two more shots." He dipped his head toward Fleurette's blue ball, still resting out of position beyond the third wicket. A fleeting smile crossed Leora's face, and Kellen bit back a laugh. He'd bet she'd just figured out how to win at this game.

Sure enough, she used Fleurette's blue ball to gain another free shot, then clunked her own ball toward her next goal. Using her unorthodox technique, Leora had overtaken both Careen and Fleurette in a single turn.

Behind the sixth wicket, Sol Stanton lit up his pipe and frowned into a haze of blue smoke. Hank Morehouse was gazing at Miss Mayfield with adoration.

Kellen silently cheered her on. She had guts.

But no matter what she tried, or how artfully she played from then on, she couldn't catch Fleurette or Careen. The game ended when Fleurette rallied and gained her thirty-second point for the first-round victory.

"First match to Miss LeClair," Josh announced. "Time for refreshments."

The storekeeper caught up to Lolly as she headed toward the refreshment table. "You're learnin' fast, ma'am," he intoned at her side.

"Not fast enough, I'm afraid."

"Remember what I told ya about the line of fire."

Lolly bent her head to hear Joshua Bodwin's words of advice. "Yes, stay out of the line of fire. Play off your opponent's ball. Very well, I shall try...."

She raised her gaze to find Colonel Macready looking straight at her, and the expression in his eyes sent her thoughts tumbling. While the shopkeeper talked on, Lolly nodded and mmm-hmmed with not the faintest idea what he was saying.

All she could think about was the extremely odd way her body felt all of a sudden, as if it were shot through with sunlight and as floaty as a gossamer-winged butterfly. Could this be another effect of drinking applejack?

Or was it the colonel's gaze that caused her such strange and delicious distress? She was drawn to his eyes, helpless under his steady perusal of her face. She felt as if he could see deep inside her, where her secret thoughts, her secret longings lay buried.

She wrenched her attention away from him and

tried to listen to Mr. Bodwin. If she met Kellen's eyes, the storekeeper's continuing explanations were simply disjointed buzzing in her ears. And if she *didn't* meet his eyes?

She purposely focused on the glass of lemonade that had appeared in her hand and listened as hard as she could, but the storekeeper's words danced into her brain and just as quickly skittered away. Her mind had flown somewhere else.

Deliberately she kept her eyes down, watched the drops of condensation roll down the sides of the tall glass she held. But she could not stop thinking about the colonel's calm, knowing eyes and the havoc they were playing with her equilibrium.

Her knees were beginning to feel soft and squishy, like farmer's cheese. Struggling to control her ragged breathing, she resolved she would never, never touch applejack again!

During the next round Lolly managed to keep up with the other two players better than she had at first. Careen won the second game, and Fleurette pouted over her extra-sugared lemonade until play resumed for the final game.

By the third and final round, a sweet-smelling cloud of Sol's pipe smoke hung over the green, Minnie Sullivan had taken over Dora Mae's paper fan and Kellen guessed Hank Morehouse had fallen out of love with Miss Mayfield and into love with Miss LeClair. Hank played on the Maple Falls baseball team, and he admired winners.

Carrie's shots were brilliant. Leora Mayfield desperately tried to emulate the strategies and techniques demonstrated on the field, but she finished dead last in every round. In the end, it was Fleurette who won the match by a single stroke. The colonel congratulated her and moved on.

When the mallets and balls were rounded up and returned, the three women instinctively gathered together in the dogwood grove.

"Ladies, Ah thank y'all for a good morning's sport," Fleurette drawled to her two companions.

"You don't suppose…" Carrie began in a thoughtful tone. "You don't suppose it really *matters* to the colonel whether we are athletically inclined?"

Lolly said the only sensible thing that came to mind. "Why should it matter? Wives in Kansas, or in Oregon, don't have time to play croquet."

Fleurette's golden eyebrows arched. "Well, Ah declare. Don't you Yankee women know anything about—" she lowered her voice to a whisper "—bein' in bed with a man? A husband, Ah mean?"

Lolly studied Fleurette's peaches-and-cream

face. She could not possibly be speaking from experience. Or could she?

"Would you be so kind as to explain such matters to us...Yankees?" She used her Pacify the Enemy tone; more than once it had saved her skin
from an angry crowd of pro-slavers in Baxter
Springs. Perhaps it would prove effective out here
in Oregon.

"Well, Ah will tell y'all what mah mammy told
me. She said the romantical part came first, and
that didn't take much more than a smile and a
promise. But the athletic part, that part comes after
the romantical, and..." She took a long, slow sip
of her lemonade.

"And?" Carrie and Lolly echoed together.

"And it—the Act, Ah mean—requires a good
deal of stamina."

"What is it they do that requires stamina?" Carrie asked in a hushed voice.

Fleurette sipped again. Carrie fidgeted with the
blue bow nestled in her shiny brown upswept
hairdo. Lolly wondered if Fleurette was pulling
their legs.

"Well, there's some turnin' over in bed to get
into position...and then there's kissin' and touchin'
all over and—"

Carrie snorted. "That can't take much stamina. All you'd have to do is lie there and kiss back!"

"Y'all didn't let me finish," Fleurette purred. "After the kissin' and touchin' comes the thrustin'. That's the part that's athletic, along with the heavin' and sweatin' and cryin' out that goes with it."

Carrie blushed to the roots of her hairline. "Have you ever experienced it? The athletic part?"

Fleurette's cheeks colored from peach to rose. "Mercy, no. Why Ah'd be ruined if Ah had. Things might be less straitlaced out here in the West, but down in N'Awlins, even a breath of scandal can ruin a girl's prospects."

"Seems like it'd be an awful long time from the romantic part to the athletic part," Carrie observed in a matter-of-fact tone. "Why even *think* about it now?"

Fleurette's green eyes widened. "Don't y'all want to be ready? Ah do. Ah most certainly do. Why, Ah do special exercises each and every night in preparation. The early bird gets the worm, remember?"

Carrie laid her hand on Fleurette's dimity-swathed forearm. "I don't think Colonel Macready would care much for thrusting and sweating."

"Why, honey, he's a man, isn't he? Course he

cares. Ah can *make* him care.'' A heated, secretive look came into the green eyes. She uttered the words with such vehemence, such supreme confidence, Lolly wondered what else Fleurette knew about men.

Whatever it was, she wasn't telling.

"Oh, look," Carrie said. "Here comes Dora Mae and Minnie." She waved. "Over here, Mrs. Landsfelter."

"Halloo!" Dora Mae sailed toward them in a purple-flowered day dress. Minnie's hands flitted from chest to nose and back. "We have some good news," she called.

"I'll tell it, Minnie. You'll get it all mixed up."

"No, I won't, Dora Mae. I have it all perfectly straight in my head."

Dora Mae swooped to a stop before their little circle and surveyed them with an unusually wide smile. "You ladies will simply never guess what is going to happen tomorrow!"

"A Bramble Scramble?" Fleurette rolled her eyes toward the upper branches of the dogwood arbor. "What in heaven's name is that?"

"That's Dora Mae Landsfelter's name for the treasure hunt she holds every summer. Everyone in town participates,'' Carrie said. ''Except this year it will be just the three of us.''

''A treasure hunt!'' Fleurette clapped her hands. ''What absolute fun!''

''And a challenge. Some years, people have even gotten lost,'' Carrie said.

''Lost?'' Lolly asked.

Carrie shrugged. ''Oh, you know how men are about following other people's directions. Especially a woman's. Every year someone loses their way and doesn't get back until after midnight.''

''What kind of directions?'' Fleurette asked with a slight tremor in her voice.

''Well, Dora Mae adores poetry. All the directions are written in rhyming verse.''

''Verse? You mean written out in poetry?''

''Printed, actually. Dora Mae does it herself the night before the Scramble.''

Fleurette went suddenly still.

Before she could stop herself, Lolly glanced at Fleurette. Why would someone who was young, beautiful, exquisitely dressed and from an apparently socially prominent Southern family offer herself as a bride in a small, unexciting town like Maple Falls, Oregon? Lolly's news reporter-trained nose fairly twitched with curiosity, but the high-pitched whistle of a locomotive reined in her thoughts.

Her trunk! Her clothes!

"Excuse me, Mrs. Landsfelter, I'm wanted at the train station."

She hated to leave without discovering why Fleurette had come out to Oregon in the first place. *Without discovering what a Bramble Scramble was.* But the thought of donning proper garments overrode everything else.

An hour later, Hank Morehouse and two freckle-faced young friends carted Lolly's trunk up to her hotel room, accepted the nickels she doled out to each of them and clattered down the stairs.

Lolly gazed at the big black rectangle. *That box holds all the possessions I have in this world.* All of them. Everything she couldn't fit into the trunk, she'd sold, including the newspaper office and everything in it—her father's oak desk, the letter-press, typesetting trays, even the scrap barrel.

Now what? She'd cut her ties and burned her bridges behind her. There was nowhere she could go but forward.

She shook out her four high-necked day dresses in restrained shades of blue and gray and her sturdy sateen work skirts and hung them up in the armoire alongside three plain white waists and her Sunday petticoat. She propped her hands on her hips and with a sigh studied the contents of her wardrobe for a long minute.

Every single article looked…serviceable. No lace. No ruffles. No ribbon rosette trimmings. She didn't own one item with any feminine furbelows. Compared with Fleurette's frills-and-feathers approach to garbing herself, Lolly was the plainest of Janes. Even prim schoolmarm Carrie Gundersen showed more flair for dressing attractively.

''Why,'' she said aloud to the armoire, ''would a man give me even a second glance?''

What does Colonel Macready see when he looks at me?

At the thought, she sighed again and tried to put the field worker's straw hat and oversize man's shirt she wore out of her mind. Where was her beribboned afternoon hat? Her white go-to-meeting gloves? She bent to dig deep into the bowels of the lavender-scented trunk.

The next time the colonel laid his eyes on her she would look suitably garbed, groomed and altogether glorious! She wanted him to notice her. She wanted him to *like* her!

For heaven's sake, Lolly, admit it. You want the colonel to marry you!

But that was getting ahead of herself. Two other

females, younger and prettier than she, wanted exactly the same thing. She would try her best to be the one selected, but the best woman—*oh, horrors, surely not the most athletic?*—would win.

Perching on the chair by the open window, Lolly pushed aside the sheer muslin curtain and looked out on the town. She liked Maple Falls. The main street was not windswept and dusty like the rutted streets were in Kansas. Children in pinafores and coveralls played Run Sheep Run in the town square, their high voices floating on the breeze.

The stores and businesses on both sides of the street looked neat and well cared for. Judging by the gleam of the buildings in the afternoon sunlight, some of the outer walls had been recently painted.

Best of all, no rowdies were storming the newspaper office. Here no gang of ruffians threatened her life, or her livelihood. Here, she thought with a spurt of gladness, women who worked for a living weren't looked down on. Even Dora Mae Landsfelter's daughter-in-law sewed ladies' garments for a living and no one objected, except for the owner of Bodwin's Mercantile, and he had a good business reason.

This was as close to heaven as she'd ever been. Instead of flat gray plains, green-cloaked hills protected serene valleys bathed in gold light. The Oregon trees grew lush and tall, unbowed by constant wind off the hot, dry plains. And the air... She drew in a huge lungful. The air smelled of baking bread and damp, fertile earth.

She closed her eyes. She could grow roses. Sweet William. Daffodils in the spring!

Oh, God, I want to belong in this pretty, peaceful town.

But to do that, she had to win the competition.

Chapter Seven

Mrs. Squires elbowed open the door into the colonel's study and placed the overloaded tray on a side table. "There, now, Colonel. Three dozen roast beef sandwiches and far too much whiskey, if ye ask me."

Kellen looked up from the desk. "Thank you, Madge."

"When do ye expect your gentlemen friends?"

He glanced at the mantel clock. "Any minute now. You needn't stay, Madge. I'll wash up later."

His housekeeper propped her hands on her bony hips. "Ye won't like bein' married, Colonel. Yer too used to doin' for yourself."

"You're probably right," he said. But it wasn't the "doin'," as Mrs. Squires put it, that he minded. It was the "being." Married people spent time in each other's company. Married people were expected to love each other. The last thing on earth Kellen wanted was an ensnared heart.

Mrs. Squires hesitated in the open doorway. "It's frustratin', it is, when you've lived as long as I have and you know all the answers, but nobody bothers to ask you the questions."

Kellen laughed. "What should I ask?" He rose and took the woman's freckled hand. "I don't know what questions to ask," he repeated in a quiet tone.

"Stayed a bachelor too long, that's what I say." She brushed an imaginary bit of fluff off Kellen's cheek. "Och, ye haven't shaved, now have ye? Must be no ladies comin', then."

"No ladies. Just Sol Stanton and Mr. Tillotsen, as usual."

"Good night to ye, then, laddie. See you don't make a mess in my kitchen."

Kellen grinned at the woman. Mrs. Squires was worse, in some ways, than his mother had been. And better in others. Madge Squires had lived through the war; Adeline Macready had died of pneumonia that first winter.

At the stroke of eight, the tap of a walking stick at the front door alerted him to Sol Stanton's arrival. For over a decade, the three men had gathered every Wednesday to play cards and exchange news. Orven was usually late because his newspaper went to press on Wednesday afternoon and he couldn't leave the shop until the last copy was printed and folded.

Orven's lateness didn't bother Kellen. It was the company he valued, the frankness among men he'd known ever since he'd come to Maple Falls. The cigars. The camaraderie. The talk, usually about women. Tonight Kellen had something specific on his mind.

"Sol." He reached to shake the man's hand. "Come in."

"Orven's just turning the corner," Sol said. "He's got a wild look in his eye. You got any whiskey?"

Two hours later, the sandwiches had disappeared and the whiskey was running low. Kellen shuffled the deck for the third time in as many minutes and started to deal another hand, but Sol stopped him.

"I've had enough poker for one night," he said. "Let's talk some."

Orven Tillotsen reached for the cut-crystal whiskey decanter. "What's on your mind, Sol?"

"Women."

"Now, that's a surprise," Kellen joked. "Understanding women is like nailing soap bubbles to a tree.''

''Don't have to understand them to, well, uh, admire them.''

''Them?'' Kellen caught his friend's eye. ''How many women do you have on your admiration list, Orv?''

Orven frowned. ''Just one in particular.''

''One at a time, you mean?'' Sol suggested. Both the older men enjoyed joshing the young newspaper editor. Sol lit his pipe and puffed blue smoke into the already hazy atmosphere of Kellen's study. ''Something on your mind, Orv?''

''Yeah, I guess so. It's about this bride business. You're a smart man, Kelly. Why'd you go for Dora Mae's idea in the first place. It's kinda like getting a potluck bride.''

Kellen surveyed his friends. ''Age doesn't necessarily bring wisdom, Sol. Sometimes it just brings...*age.*''

Sol chuckled. ''And that means?''

''I'm feeling old, gentlemen.''

''Well, hell,'' Sol spluttered. ''Who isn't?''

The newspaper editor swelled out his chest. ''I'm not.''

''Orven, you're thirty-four, for God's sake. Still wet behind the ears.''

"I'm old enough to—" He broke off and up-ended his whiskey glass.

"And," Kellen continued, "maybe I'm a bit... lonely."

"Lonely!" Sol roared. "Dammit, man, you could have any female in this town. If you're lonely, it's your own fault."

Orven shook his head. "Maybe he doesn't want just *any* female."

"Yeah?" Sol turned to Kellen with a grin. Which one *do* you want?"

Again, Kellen studied his two friends. "The truth?"

"The truth," Sol and Orven said together.

"The truth is it doesn't much matter. That's why I went along with Dora Mae's idea. I loved some-one once, Sol. I lost her and it damn near killed me. I don't ever intend to do so again."

"Care to make a wager?" Sol stuck out his hand. "Fifty bucks says you'll lose your heart, *then* you'll get married. Dora Mae or no Dora Mae."

"Not me," Kellen said carefully. "Fifty bucks says I won't," Kellen said with a smile. He shook Sol's extended hand. "Orven, you want in on this?"

"You crazy?"

"Crazy? No. Just old enough to be realistic."

Orven sniffed. "By the way, you got any more whiskey?"

"How about some of Josh Bodwin's special-brewed applejack?" Kellen offered.

Instantly two empty glasses slid across the table toward him, and then all three men laughed, settled back in their chairs, and talked about women, horses and politics, in that order, until long past midnight.

"Well? What does it say?" Carrie and Fleurette pressed in, peering over Lolly's shoulders as she unfolded the square of paper in her hand. Next to them on the hotel veranda stood the three Ladies Helpful Society members.

Dora Mae Landsfelter, in a royal-blue afternoon dress and a hat with a blue peacock feather that bobbed at her every commanding gesture, waited impatiently while Lolly smoothed open the note containing the first clue in the treasure hunt she called a Bramble Scramble. Ruth Underwood stood quietly to one side, her smooth round face and girlish figure belying her years; and Minnie Sullivan, dressed in a flounced green check gingham, fluttered her hands like butterflies around her green bonnet.

Townspeople milled on the board sidewalk in

front of the hotel, jingling quarters into Minnie's Bramble Scramble collection jar.

Lolly glanced down at the paper and read aloud the carefully printed words. "'Across the street and in the square, you will find the first clue there.'"

Carrie danced a little jig at her side. "The first clue! Oh, hurry, let's go and find it!"

Fleurette looked suddenly uncertain. "Let's?" she repeated. "As in 'let *us*'?"

"Yes! Come on!"

"Y'all really mean *us?* All of us together?"

Lolly understood in an instant. "She's right, Carrie. Before we start, the three of us must decide something."

She reached out her arms and drew both women in closer until they stood in a bell-skirted huddle. Heads bent, they looked like a multicolored three-petaled flower. Fleurette in pale pink, Carrie in printed lilac and Lolly in a dark-blue sateen skirt and white waist instead of the black travel outfit she'd worn since she arrived in Maple Falls.

She looked down at the six shoes, arranged in a rough circle on the veranda floor. How different they all were. One tiny pair of flimsy pink slippers, one pair of shiny leather button-ups and Lolly's old, comfortable Sensible Shoes, as she called them. She'd dug them out of her trunk an hour earlier, clutching them to her chest like an old friend.

She lifted her head and addressed Carrie and Fleurette.

"Ladies? Shall we work as a team, even though it is a competition? That is, put our heads together to gather the clues? Or is it to be every woman for herself?"

A long minute of silence passed before Fleurette's soft, well-modulated voice posed a further question. "If weah all workin' together, how can just one of us win the scramble?"

Carrie clapped her hands in delight. "We could award the points to ourselves! On the honor system. I use it in my teaching, and it's ever so successful. It would be so much more fun to do the scramble together, don't you think?"

"Whoever actually discovers the clue would be awarded the point, is that it?" Lolly said. "And at the end we would—"

"Of course! It's just perfect," Carrie burbled. "Dora Mae may have created the scramble, but *we* can decide how best to proceed. And *we* can choose the winner!"

Lolly could guess why Carrie's students liked her; she was as enthusiastic and young spirited as a frisky colt. Surely she would wish to continue teaching, even if she did marry Colonel Macready.

"Are we agreed, then?" Lolly asked. "We will band together for the scramble?"

"Goodness, yes," Carrie chirped. "Three heads arc surely better than one!"

After a pause, Fleurette smiled. "Theah is strength in numbers."

"All right, then." Lolly grinned at them. "We shall be like the Three Musketeers."

Fleurette looked puzzled for a moment, then her expression reverted to a practiced smile. With an airy wave of her hand, she turned to Lolly. "Then we'd best better hurry on over to the park. The crowd's gettin' so thick, y'all won't be able to see a thing 'cept arms and legs."

The three women straightened, then parted and marched across the street, arms linked. "All for one, and one for all!" Carrie sang.

"Oh, weah bein' so silly!"

Carrie poked an elbow into Fleurette's pink bodice. "Yes, but isn't it fun?"

"Besides," Lolly said in her logical tone, "we really do need each other. Carrie is the only one who knows the countryside!"

The three women combed the square, inspected the trees, poked through the grass, brushed aside pale-pink peonies and black-eyed Susans to peer beneath stones. No clues.

Finally, a perspiring Lolly sought the shade of the maple, reached into her skirt pocket and unfolded the rhyme. *In the square.* "In the square *what?*" she said aloud.

Instantly the women reassembled around her. Fleurette spoke first. "Doesn't the square mean the town park? The *town* square?"

"Wait!" Carrie yelped. "Maybe we should look for something square in shape."

"Exactly! Like a brick or a pavin' stone or a...?"

"Sign!" Lolly said suddenly. "Look!" She pointed to the square metal sign posted on the street corner. Maple Falls, Population 983.

"That's it!" Carrie breathed. "It has to be." She raced through clustered onlookers, stretched on tiptoe as tall as she could, and teetered off balance. Orven Tillotsen stepped out of the crowd to steady her with a hand at her back.

"Thank you, Orven," Carrie managed with a blush. She plucked a square of paper off the back side of the sign, and the townspeople murmured and applauded.

Again the three women bent their heads together while Carrie read the second clue aloud. "'Among the green and red and blue, lies the second clever clue.' "

Fleurette sniffed. "Green and red and blue? What a perfectly dreadful color combination."

"For summer frocks, perhaps," Lolly said. "But maybe this is for something else. Flowers? Bachelor buttons are blue."

"And red roses grow on Minnie Sullivan's front fence," Carrie chimed in.

"But…"

"Down in N'Awlins y'all never find those colors togetheh in one place unless…" An odd light came into Fleurette's green eyes.

"Unless what?" Carrie said.

"Where?" Lolly pressed on.

Fleurette hesitated, as if weighing something in her mind. After a full minute, Lolly pinned her with a look.

"Well?"

The younger woman swallowed. "Oh, all right. Ah'll show you."

She led the way down one tree-shaded street, up another and through the scrolled iron gate into Colonel Macready's backyard. Without pausing Fleurette headed straight across yesterday's croquet court and down to the river's edge, the crowd surging behind at a respectful distance.

"Y'all see 'em?" Fleurette pointed to the neat wooden dock. "Boats. Down home all the shrimp boats are painted bright colors, so I thought…"

Carrie hugged her. "You are exactly right! Rowboats!

One green one, one red one and two blue ones! Fleurette, you are very clever!"

A strange look came over Fleurette's face, a curious mix of surprise and hesitant, shy pride. Lolly was used to seeing pride in the young woman's expression, but shyness?

There was some mystery about the woman; she could practically smell it.

Fleurette escaped Lolly's probing gaze and flew down to the dock at the river's edge. Sure enough, lodged between the cedar planks was another folded square of paper.

"I found it!" Fleurette held it up in triumph.

"What does it say?" Carrie called.

Fleurette's face changed so subtly, Lolly almost missed it. She watched the younger woman step off the end of the dock and come toward them, the still-folded paper in her hand.

"You read it." She thrust the note into Lolly's hand. "Weah all in this togetheh, like you said. We are sharin' the clues."

Lolly smoothed open the creased paper and eyed

the printing. "'Look to bird dog's woody tree, to seek and find clue number three.'"

"Oh, mercy," Carrie groaned. "I know nothing about dogs."

"It's not about dogs, silly." Fleurette almost giggled. "It's about a tree. A 'woody' tree."

A light went on in Lolly's head. "A *dogwood* tree."

But which one? There must be hundreds near here."

"The 'bird dog's woody tree,' Carrie quoted. "Why, that's right here! Sam, Colonel Macready's retriever, is the best bird dog in the county. And his favorite…"

"Dogwood tree?" Fleurette ventured.

"Grows in the arbor where Mrs. Squires served lemonade yesterday," Carrie announced. "Come on!"

The crowd buzzed over the spectacle of the three ladies, arms linked, flying across the grass toward the dogwood arbor where Sam was taking a nap. Sol Stanton and Kellen Macready stood off to one side, watching; Orven Tillotsen kept his worshipful gaze glued on Careen Gundersen; and Sol's pipe smoke wrapped them all in a cloud of pungent blue air.

Kellen shook his head. He had no idea what Dora Mae had in mind. But when the three competing ladies appeared, with Mrs. Landsfelter lumbering across the lawn behind them, her peacock feather swaying, Sam rose and stood at attention, neck hair bristling.

What the—? Instinctively Kellen moved forward. Good God, was Sam part of this caper?

He wasn't worried about Sam; his concern centered on anyone who might get too close to the animal. Sam didn't much take to people who didn't smell familiar.

But good Lord, there was Dora Mae's feathered hat fluttering toward the best hunting dog in the county.

Sol removed the pipe from his mouth. "Stop twitching, Kell. She'll get there."

"That's what I'm worried about. If it's anybody but Careen, Sam will run her to ground and sit on her."

Sol laughed. "Can't wait to see that. Especially if it's that little Southern filly."

Kellen quirked one eyebrow at his friend. "Might lose my dog in all those petticoats."

Sol gestured across the lawn with his pipe. "Might lose him anyway when he flushes Dora Mae's hat!"

The trio halted and gathered into what looked to Kellen like a multicolored knot. Minutes went by as they alternately whispered together and looked over at Sam under the dogwood arbor.

Then, very slowly, the figure clad in a froth of pale pink started toward the animal. Beside Kellen, Sol Stanton stiffened.

Fleurette LeClair edged toward the arbor, her pink shoes disappearing into the lush grass. When Sam took a tentative step toward her, she began talking. Kellen couldn't hear the words, but he hoped to God she knew what she was doing.

"Dammit, Kell, stop her!"

"Sam!" The dog hesitated, looked toward Kellen, then back to Fleurette, one foot raised.

The young woman inched forward another step, reached out her hand. The dog went into a trembly crouch.

Sol Stanton stuffed his pipe into his vest pocket and started forward. At that same instant Sam leaped.

The animal shot past Fleurette, knocking her to her knees, and threw himself at Dora Mae Landsfelter's peacock-feathered hat. It sailed off her head to the ground, and Sam plopped his front paws on top of it.

The crowd roared with laughter.

"Sam!" Kellen yelled. "Heel!"

Careen Gundersen darted forward, Leora Mayfield at her elbow. While the dog batted Dora Mae's hat into a pancake and cheers punctuated the spectators' guffaws, Careen and Leora raced toward Miss LeClair.

Sol's laughter slowed Kellen down. If Stanton was laughing, no one was injured. It wouldn't be like Sol to gain amusement from someone else's pain or embarrassment. Unless, he reminded himself, it was Dora Mae Landsfelter. Privately, Sol referred to her as "Attila the Nun," even though she'd been married almost forty years.

Sol reached Miss LeClair first and helped her to her feet while Careen rescued the peacock feather hat. Leora Mayfield presented it to Mrs. Landsfelter, spoke a few words and suddenly the two were hugging each other and smiling. At least Dora Mae was smiling; Kellen couldn't see Leora's face.

Sol escorted Miss LeClair to the safety of the dogwood arbor, while Careen tried to pacify Sam by rubbing his neck. Then the figure in pink raised one delicate-looking arm and pointed.

"Carrie, look what's tied under his collar!"

Carrie felt under Sam's leather collar with her fingers, pulled out a bit of paper rolled into a narrow tube. The onlookers instantly fell silent.

Fleurette skimmed over the grass and snatched the roll while Carrie held onto Sam.

"What's the clue?" Hank Morehouse yelled from the sidelines.

With trembling hands Fleurette unrolled the paper and stared at it. Carrie stood on tiptoe craning to see over her shoulder. Leora leaned forward to hear, and Dora Mae Landsfelter gave her a gentle nudge. "You go on, now, Miss Mayfield. You don't want to miss out. The hidden treasure is, well, a real treasure."

Sol strolled back across the lawn with a grin on his craggy face. "That's some woman," he remarked.

Kellen nodded. "Agreed."

"She's got spunk." Sol held Kellen's eyes.

"And she's as good-looking as they come."

"What do you think, Orv?" Sol spoke over his shoulder to the newspaper editor. Kellen watched the younger man's eyes glaze over. "She's got... everything."

"Shhhh!" someone interjected. "They're gonna read the clue out loud."

Fleurette's trembling hand stuffed the paper into Carrie's palm. "You read it."

Carrie's schoolteacher's voice carried easily to the far reaches of Colonel Macready's backyard.

"'Look not west for clue the fourth. And neither look east, south or north.'"

Carrie looked up, her brown eyes puzzled. "Well, my heavens, what can that mean? Leora? Fleurette?"

The three looked at each other while Dora Mae Landsfelter signaled the other two Helpful Ladies, who smiled and smiled as if they had all swallowed a cage full of canaries.

"Obviously, it's a riddle," Lolly said at last.

Fleurette shrugged. "Badly worded. The rhythm is off, y'all hear it?"

"Hush!" Carrie cautioned. "Dora Mae will hear you."

"Ah'm so sorry," Fleurette whispered. "Ah must mind mah manners."

Lolly blinked. Sorry? Manners? Since when did Fleurette pay any mind to manners? Then again, now that she thought about it, Fleurette had been almost polite this morning, even helpful ever since the three of them had embarked on the scramble together.

How very curious. What could possibly be the reason for this sudden change? Right before Lolly's eyes, Fleurette was becoming almost…likable. Well, more human, at any rate.

Was there something Fleurette *needed* from them?

Chapter Eight

Carrie's puzzled voice brought Lolly back to the problem at hand. "Not west or east or south or north. That must mean...?"

"Right where we-all are standin'!"

"Or would be, if we'd found Sam under his dogwood tree."

Three pairs of eyes turned toward the shaded arbor where the retriever had lain. "Leora, you look," Carrie urged. "So far, you have no points at all."

Lolly's jaw dropped. "Why, you goose, don't you want to win the prize? And the colonel?" she added in a softer tone.

"Why, of course I do! But I'm ahead by two points, and Fleurette already has one win from yesterday. You don't have any. According to the law of averages..."

Lolly laid a hand on Carrie's arm. "Why, you dear girl, averages have nothing to do with it. You just want everybody to be happy, don't you?"

"Not at all!" Carrie flared. "I mean I just thought you'd feel better if—"

Lolly's heart melted into a puddle of vanilla pudding. "Don't you waste your time, or your scramble points, on me. I am older than both of you, and maybe even smarter and meaner and..."

"Oh, but you're not!" Carrie protested. "Well, maybe you're a tiny bit older, but—"

"If weah evah goin' to solve this riddle, we should stop bein' so nicey-nice to each other and *think*." Fleurette's cheeks turned rose, then deepened to crimson. "Ah mean to win that treasure-prize, *and* the colonel. So let's stick to business."

Well! That was more like the old Fleurette. For some reason Lolly felt at ease with that. She didn't know what to make of the other Fleurette.

"We must think!" Lolly urged. "Not west, east, north or south from the arbor must mean the clue is...*in* the arbor!"

"And the first one theah wins the point!" Fleurette pivoted and started for the dogwood grove.

Leora Mayfield glided up to the arbor, not even breathing hard, and while the other two females stood panting for air, Leora tipped her head back, reached into the low-drooping dogwood branches and pulled out a paper packet tied with a bit of string.

Carrie regained her wind first. "Read it, Leora."

"Then Ah simply must have some lemonade!" Fleurette puffed beside her, her cheeks as pink as her dress.

Lolly cleared her throat and opened her lips. "'The final clue will guide you to...the prize, behind a door of blue.'"

"A blue door? Wheah would that be, do y'all suppose? Carrie?"

"Well, there's Matthew Underwood's barn. It's got a big blue door."

"Is it far?"

Carrie sighed. "On Grove Street. The other side of town."

"Oh, no," two voices groaned in unison.

"Ah can't. Ah simply can't."

Lolly silently agreed. "We must. Carrie, you've won the most points. It's plain to see you will win the Scramble prize. You must claim it."

"Not until we've had some refreshment," Carrie pronounced. "Agreed?"

Lolly and Fleurette nodded.

"Lemonade, then. At the hotel."

The trio linked arms and marched back toward

town, followed by a straggly crowd of towns-people.

An hour later, after a short rest and gallons of lemonade, they set off again. This time their destination was straight to Matthew Underwood's barn.

The barn sat amidst a field of lavender behind a peaceful looking two-story house on Grove Street. "Mrs. Underwood grows lavender for sachets," Carrie explained.

Lolly breathed in the pungent scent and smiled. Ruth Underwood had enough lavender to perfume the entire town.

She gazed across the nodding sea of purple blooms to the barn in the sweet-smelling meadow. Sure enough, it had a wide double door painted so blue it looked like the summer sky.

Ignoring the crowd that followed them, the two women followed Carrie down the lavender-bordered path and lined up at the barn entrance.

"Should we knock?" Fleurette asked.

"Don't be silly, it's a *barn.*" Carrie pulled open the door and peeked inside. "Mr. Underwood keeps his cultivator and his plow inside, and feed for his cow."

"Halloo, Mr. Underwood?" After a moment she shrugged. "He's not here. Let's go inside."

Carrie led the way into the dim interior. Warm, musty air swirled into Lolly's nostrils and she took a deep breath. It smelled nothing at all like Kansas.

"Such an odd place for a treasure hunt," Fleurette murmured. "Unless…"

"Unless what?" Carrie said. "Oh, you mean unless the prize is…"

The three looked at each other. "Alive," they murmured in unison.

"Over there," Lolly whispered. "In the first stall."

A large black eye surveyed them, then two sleek, brown-tipped ears twitched and a tentative whicker floated into the quiet.

"My heavens, it's a horse!" Lolly blurted.

Fleurette clasped her hands at her bosom. "Oh, the darlin' thing!"

Carrie turned white as flour paste.

Lolly wondered if she was going to faint, but after a moment the schoolteacher sent her a wobbly smile and Lolly shifted her gaze back to the horse. "Look! There's a red ribbon tied around its neck. And a card." She reached in and slipped it free. "For the winner," she read aloud.

Fleurette squealed with excitement. "A horse? The prize is a whole horse?"

Carrie said nothing.

"My, my, isn't it a beauty? Gracious, Ah'm talkin' out of turn. It's Carrie's prize."

Carrie backed away and sat down abruptly on a bale of hay. "I don't want anything to do with it. I'm scared to death of horses."

"But..." Lolly and Fleurette stared at her.

Carrie lifted her chin. "But nothing. It's a prize I cannot accept. Therefore, I give it to you. Both of you, to share. Now each of you owns one half of this horse."

Fleurette blinked away tears. "Why, you sweet, sweet thing!" She gave Carrie a swift hug. "Just think, Leora, we own a beautiful—" she sped to the stall and ran her eyes over the animal "—mare."

"So I see." Lolly felt as if an apple had lodged in her throat.

Fleurette turned a beaming face toward her, and suddenly the green eyes narrowed. "If you cannot ride, I guess Ah'll have to teach you." With every hour that passed, Fleurette became more of a puzzle.

"I can ride," Lolly replied. "Why would you assume I could not?"

"We will take turns, then," Fleurette announced. "And now that the matter is settled, Ah propose we have some lunch. And some more lemonade. Last one to the hotel is a…''

She dashed out the barn door so fast her final words were lost. The crowd parted to let her through and cheered as she passed among them.

''She's acting like a queen on a royal progress,'' Lolly murmured from the door.

''There cannot be another surprise today,'' Carrie said in a tired voice. ''My brain is melting in this heat.''

Lolly squinted at the retreating figure in the billowy pink dress. ''I wouldn't count on that. I spy Dora Mae Landsfelter, and she is heading straight for us.''

Carrie just looked at her.

''And,'' Lolly continued, ''Dora Mae's face has that Important Announcement look written all over it.''

''Why, that's purely outrageous!'' Fleurette fluffed out the skirt and settled herself at the dining table across from Carrie and Lolly. ''Scandalous.''

''I think,'' Lolly said carefully, ''it could be better described as 'athletic.'''

''Definitely.'' Carrie's round brown eyes sparkled. ''It's kissing, and I can hardly wait to find out what it's like!''

"That's 'cause y'all have never been courted before." Fleurette inspected the moons of her long fingernails. "Ah, howeveh, am an expert in such matters."

"Just how is it you can be such an expert in such matters and still maintain your respectability?" Carrie shot back.

"Why, honey, it's terrible easy. Ah am very, very discreet."

"I am discreet, too," Carrie said. "Nobody has kissed *me* since last Christmas when Hank Morehouse caught me under his momma's mistletoe. Delpha Morehouse is my father's second cousin, and it was at her house, right under her nose, so it was all perfectly proper. And discreet."

Fleurette crooked one tawny eyebrow.

"But I have always, *always,* wished for a *real* kiss," Carrie continued, her voice taking on a dreamy softness. "A real kiss from a real gentleman."

"One gentleman in particular?" Fleurette prompted.

"Yes." Carrie sighed the word. "I can scarcely believe it's actually going to happen. Tonight, this very night, Colonel Macready is going to kiss me!"

"Colonel Macready is going to kiss all three of

us,'' Lolly reminded. "It's part three of the Helpful
Ladies' plan.

"Ah wouldn't get mah hopes up, either of you."

Hopes up! Lolly nearly choked on her tea. She
had no hopes at all, not a single one. Not only had
she never been kissed, even by a cousin under the
mistletoe, but the thought of Colonel Macready's
mouth touching hers sent a spark of white-hot
lightning up her spine. She would shake so uncon-
trollably, he wouldn't be able to find her lips! She
prayed she could get through the ordeal without
embarrassing them both.

"Why *not* get our hopes up?" Carrie's voice
tightened. "I've been dreaming of such a miracle
for seven years, ever since I was twelve years old.
My hopes are extremely up!"

"Well, darlin', the colonel strikes me as a man
of the world." Fleurette took a delicate sip from
her tall lemonade glass. "In othah words, he's
kissed women before. Lots of 'em. He'll be lookin'
for someone who knows how."

Lolly's heart squeezed at the stricken look on
Carrie's face.

"And," Fleurette continued, "*he* is choosin' the
winner of this part of the competition. Not Dora
Mae."

Carrie blanched. "I am going home right this minute and...and...practice!"

Fleurette's laughter bubbled in the quiet dining room until Lolly thought she would scream. There was no need to humiliate Carrie—or herself, for that matter. Experience might be an advantage of a sort, but there were other considerations a man like Colonel Macready might take into account.

Weren't there?

Perhaps it didn't bear analyzing, as Carrie was sure to do. Tonight they would discover if Colonel Macready preferred his kissing companion experienced or...not.

Lolly unclenched her hands. She refused to be distressed at Fleurette's air of superiority. Unlike Carrie, she would *not* go back to her hotel room to "practice."

I am what I am, she reminded herself. A reasonably intelligent female. A spinster.

An *unkissed* spinster.

Her stomach knotted. She would not apologize for her inexperience. And she wouldn't back away from the challenge, either! Today's mighty oak is just yesterday's nut that held its ground, Papa used to say. In a manner of speaking, she was yesterday's nut. And she most certainly intended to hold her ground.

Chapter Nine

In the Golden Key saloon next door to the hotel, Kellen regarded Orven and Sol over the rim of his whiskey glass. All three sat across from each other at the scarred oak table Charlie the bartender used for poker games on Saturday nights.

Sol scowled into his whiskey. "Damn, Kelly, you have all the luck."

"Think so, do you? Remember I'm the one who's dealing with Dora Mae Landsfelter."

Orven downed his shot. "Well, hell's bells, Colonel. If I was to just up and kiss a girl I'd be engaged before you could say 'Dearly beloved.'"

"Orv's right, Kell. The way you and Dora Mae have got it fixed, you get to sample three ladies in one night, but you only have to marry one. Kinda like tasting apple pie at the county fair."

Kellen poured out three more shots. "That's the deal I made with Dora." Even though he was beginning to wish he hadn't, he'd given his word, and the word of a Macready was binding.

Orven stared at him. "You're gonna spend the rest of your life with one of those ladies. How come you don't care which one?"

Kellen shifted his gaze to the painting over the polished mahogany bar. "I don't *want* to care which one," he said quietly. "My heart's damn well hardened over, and I want it to stay that way."

"But...but think what you'll be missing," Orven protested.

"I know very well what I'll be missing." He kept his face impassive, but the hand holding his shot glass trembled. Kellen set his glass on the table and stuffed his hand into his vest pocket.

Sol rapped his pipe stem against his teeth. "So you've been hurt, Kell. You can't let that scar you for life."

Kellen's gut tightened. Scar him for life? He wanted to laugh. He had welcomed the numb, dead feeling inside him for so long, it felt natural. *Not* feeling anything was...comfortable. Safe.

"You want to be a good husband, don'tcha, Kelly?" Orven spoke quickly, an odd anxiety in his voice.

Yes, he did. But he wanted companionship, not

emotional involvement. "What makes you think I won't be?"

"For one thing, your approach is about as romantic as a dry haystack."

"When you're my age, being romantic has nothing to do with it. A good husband is a steady, sensible man who is ready to settle down and shoulder responsibilities."

Sol's bushy eyebrows rose in a subtle challenge. "Is that all?"

Kellen swallowed. He'd loved Lorena so desperately he didn't think he could live without her. The depth and intensity of his feelings made him take risks he shouldn't have during the war. The medals he earned at Chancellorsville weren't so much for courage as for not being able to think clearly. In the end, Lorena had betrayed him with his closest friend.

"Look at it this way, Sol. You take a man, knit his heart up into a love knot, and he's not steady and sensible anymore. That's not good for a woman. And it's not good for a man."

Sol rolled his eyes toward the saloon ceiling. "I pity your bride, Kell. I really do. Unless she can unlock that granite rock you call a heart. By the way," he added quickly, "who's leading the competition so far?"

Orven plunked his glass onto the table. "Miss

LeClair won the croquet match—that gives her one point.'' He held up one finger. ''Miss Careen won the scramble—that's one point for her.''

''Looks like Miss Mayfield is trailing,'' Sol said in a noncommittal tone.

''Yeah.'' Orven eyed Kellen, a slight smile showing under his mustache. ''But maybe she'll catch up tonight.''

Lolly made her way down the red-painted steps of the Golden Valley Hotel and stepped along the board sidewalk toward... Well, she wasn't exactly sure where she was headed. All she knew was she couldn't stand being cooped up in her hotel room one more minute.

Of course she wasn't nervous, she told herself. Not the least little bit. Back home, after Papa had been killed and she'd taken over the newspaper, one of her *Gazette* editorials turned the town on its ear. Someone tossed a brick through the newspaper office window, and she'd walked the streets for hours to steady her nerves. Walking had worked then; it should work now.

Except that Baxter Springs had only two streets, and Maple Falls had at least a dozen. The way her body felt, all tight inside and wound up like a spring, she could walk them all and be back at the hotel in ten minutes flat.

She crossed to Grove Street and headed toward the Underwoods' barn. Maybe it would help if she talked to her horse. She owned the front half, she decided—the half with the soft, understanding eyes. Fleurette could have the rest.

Halfway up the gentle hill, she glimpsed a figure moving toward her. Her heart skipped erratically as the distance between them lessened. Then she noticed the dog trotting at his side.

Oh, no! Colonel Macready. The very last person she wished to see on this day of all days. She fought an impulse to turn and run.

Some mighty oak you'll make, a voice whispered.

"Oh, shush!" she said aloud. "Who asked you?"

You can still run. Quick, now, before he sees you.

She couldn't move. Couldn't force her legs into making a single evasive motion, even though he was now four strides away from her. Three. Two… And then he stood before her.

"Who asked me what?" He smiled at her, and her heartbeat doubled. She couldn't take her eyes off his mouth. In a few short hours he would touch his lips to hers and…then what happened? Did they "un-touch" and that was it? The whole thing couldn't take more than four seconds. Why did her heart feel as if swallows had swooped in and taken up residence?

"Miss Mayfield? Is anything amiss?"

"No." Her voice came out quavery.

Yes! I am amiss. Tumbling around inside like Russian feather-weed in a Kansas wind.

"I feel hot," she blurted. "Because of the…" Tongue-tied she looked down at her shoes, watched Sam stretch his body full-length next to the colonel's boots and lay his head on his front paws.

"Heat?" he supplied. He was watching her face, looking straight into her eyes with a glint of understanding. She moved her gaze back to his mouth. It *must* last longer than four seconds. And what did they do about their noses?

A question bubbled past her lips before she could stop it. "You're going to kiss me, aren't you!"

Surely that wasn't her voice speaking those words?

The colonel laughed softly. "Later, yes. Not right at this moment."

"Why?"

Again Kellen laughed. Her cheeks had flushed scarlet.

Seeing her discomfort, he carried on the conversation as if nothing unusual had happened. "Why later? Or why not at this moment?'' To give her time to recover, he bent to stroke Sam's head.

''I mean, why at all?'' she said.

''Because Dora Mae Landsfelter has a stronger stomach for battle than I do.''

''Battle? You're not afraid of battle. You fought in the war, didn't you?''

The irrelevance of the question amused him. ''I did, yes. However, Mrs. Landsfelter is worse than any general I ever served under.''

Her tongue slipped out to lick her lower lip. ''We feel exactly the same way!''

''We?''

''Your…brides. The other two candidates.'' Another wave of color suffused her skin. ''The ones you're supposed to kiss tonight.''

''Yes,'' he said dryly. ''It should be a very—'' he hesitated, gauging the effect of his words ''—instructive evening.''

''Actually, I think it will be better than Dora Mae's Bramble Scramble.''

''Better?'' Most women would be simpering like addled schoolgirls by now. This one simply spoke her mind. It was refreshing. And damned disconcerting.

''Better,'' she confirmed. ''More to the point, I mean. More…athletic.'' Again her gaze lingered on his mouth.

"Miss Mayfield?"

She licked her dry lips and tried to swallow. "Yes, Colonel Macready?"

"This is the most interesting conversation I have engaged in for some time."

"You are extremely easy to talk to, Colonel. As a matter of honest fact, I find myself saying whatever comes into my head, with no thought to propriety."

"Thank God," Kellen said with a laugh. "Propriety kills more good conversations than ten Dora Mae Landsfelters."

And more good lovemaking. Good God! Where had *that* come from? Kellen wondered. He had been thinking of propriety, of protecting Leora Mayfield's reputation and then, *wham!* The cannonball from nowhere, straight into his gut. Or rather, straight into his groin.

"Miss Mayfield, may Sam and I escort you safely back to your hotel?"

"No, thank you, Colonel Macready. I've discovered a shortcut through the Underwoods' lavender field. It will calm my nerves before…well, before tonight."

"Ah, yes, the ordeal."

Her eyes widened. Large purple-blue eyes they were, the color of delphiniums.

"How did you know that's what I call it?" She stared at him, so pink and flummoxed he wanted to laugh. He wanted to shake her hand for her guileless honesty.

In the next instant he wanted to kiss her. Not later, but right this minute.

Instead he spoke to his dog. "Sam. Come."

He left her at the start of the narrow path through the lavender field, watched her pick her way slowly through the purple blooms. Then he whistled to Sam and walked straight to the Golden Valley Hotel.

He wasn't sure why he felt compelled to do this. Maybe because it was the gentlemanly thing to do, make sure she returned safely.

Something inside him rejected that thought almost immediately. His gut instinct told him it had more to do with something else. Something he couldn't exactly put his finger on.

He waited on the hotel veranda for an hour, nursing a whiskey and wondering why it was taking her so long to return. A better question might be why couldn't he stop thinking about her in the first place? He sipped his whiskey and tried not to think about it.

At last he saw her far down the boardwalk, moving slowly toward the hotel. Kellen watched until he knew she would recognize him if she came any closer, then rose from his lookout and slipped away unseen.

"The rules of engagement, so to speak, are the following." Dora Mae Landsfelter's piercing voice brought a speedy hush to the crowd of townspeople thronged in the town square. She stood on the podium before the ironwork gazebo, her head crowned with a new hat. This one, Lolly noted with an inward giggle, sported dried flowers instead of a feather.

From her perch on the bench facing the gazebo, she scanned the park for Sam and exhaled in relief when she saw no sign of the animal.

Or the colonel. Had he backed out of this kissing ordeal?

"The first rule," Dora Mae announced in a voice ringing with authority, "regards speaking. Once inside the gazebo, neither the candidate nor the colonel may speak. This will ensure a completely unbiased assessment of the…er…event."

"Ya mean the *kiss,* don'tcha, Miz Landsfelter?" a young male voice called.

The elderly woman drew herself up. "Henry Morehouse, you hush up this instant or you will be ejected from the proceedings."

"I paid my quarter! Don't I git to watch?"

Dora Mae pointed a long forefinger into the crowd. "You behave yourself, you young rapscallion!"

"The second rule," she continued in an agitated tone, "applies to Colonel Macready. At his request, he will be blindfolded to ensure the anonymity of each candidate."

"*We* know who they are," Delpha Morehouse remarked.

Dora Mae coughed discreetly. "Of course. But at the time of the…um…assessment, the colonel will not."

"Ya mean the kiss, huh, Miz— Awright, awright, I'm goin!'

Dora Mae pressed on over the ripples of laughter accompanying the Morehouse boy's sudden exit. "Third, as you can see, thanks to the seamstress skills of my daughter-in-law, Hulda Jane Landsfelter, the gazebo has been completely curtained for privacy."

"Ya mean the colonel and lady he's kissin'?" came a faint cry from across the street.

Sol Stanton detached himself from the onlookers and set off in the direction of the voice. Dora Mae continued with an angry twitch of the dried poppies on her hat. Lolly had to admire the woman's composure under the circumstances. Her own nerves were strung tight as a clothesline wire.

"There will be no peeking or other interruption during the—"

"Kiss— Ow! Leggo of me!" came a muffled wail.

"Event," Dora Mae finished.

Lolly choked down a blurp of nervous laughter and felt a bubble of air work its way down her gullet. *Oh, please God, not the hiccups. Not tonight. I'll do anything. I'll say my prayers every single night. I'll...give my half of the horse to Fleurette!*

The thought was so startling that the air bubble evaporated. Instantly Lolly considered her offer concerning the horse. She *liked* that horse.

"Remember, ladies." Dora Mae nodded toward the scrolled iron bench beneath the maple tree where Lolly sat between Fleurette and Carrie. "You are not to speak to the colonel."

The crowd shuffled with restless energy. Lolly squirmed, then forced her attention back to Dora Mae's voice.

"Are the candidates ready to draw straws for position?"

"They're ready!" the townspeople roared.

Lolly felt hot all over and so jittery inside she imagined bumblebees dancing the polka with a horde of butterflies. She shot a glance at Fleurette, sitting at the far end of the bench. Any man with half an eye could see how soft and feminine and elegant the young Southern woman appeared in her peach silk dress. The tight ringlets shimmered with golden light, and her face…

Why of all things! Fleurette looked maddeningly sure of herself!

Lolly gritted her teeth. No, she was not jealous. Not. Not. *Not.*

Well, maybe just a little.

Deliberately she straightened her backbone, drew in a slow, calming breath and tried to smile. Surely she wasn't too old to learn how to be attractive to a man? Maybe she could even take a lesson or two from the beautiful and experienced Fleurette?

"What's the matter?" Carrie whispered. "You look like you're going to the guillotine, not into the gazebo with the colonel."

"I'm…I'm…I can't tell you."

Carrie sent her a sympathetic look and squeezed Lolly's arm. "He's not going to know it's *you*, remember?"

Oh, but he would. He couldn't help it. Even if she uttered not one syllable, he would hear her heart beating, just like that night at the reception. Just like this afternoon on Grove Street.

He would know how green she was. How scared and unready and inept she felt.

Dora Mae approached with three straws in her closed hand. Lolly closed her eyes and selected one.

The shortest one. She would go last. Last, of all things! The colonel would be jaded with kisses by that time. His lips would be so numb he wouldn't feel a thing.

Pull yourself together, Lolly! She had stood up to rowdy farmers in Kansas. Even bandits. She had faced rifles pointed at her heart. Why was she so frightened of a simple little kiss?

Her heart seemed to curl in on itself. She knew only one thing for certain; she would go crazy with waiting.

Fleurette's dainty white hand plucked the longest straw. Brandishing it like a scepter, she rose and fluffed out her ruffly skirt. Lolly fumed in silence. Fleurette had changed her clothes, again; that made three times today! Now she wore that elegant afternoon dress of peach organza, and she smelled—Lolly sniffed the air in her wake—like lily of the valley. Even blindfolded, Colonel Macready would be smitten just by drawing in a breath!

Fleurette floated up the steps and past the gazebo curtains. The restless crowd fell silent.

Beside her, Carrie grasped her hand. ''Don't frown so, Leora. One would think you've gone green-eyed with jealousy.''

"Well, I haven't," Lolly whispered back. *Oh, yes, you have,* an inner voice contradicted.

"No," she said aloud, her tone resolute. "I have not."

Carrie's smile was so understanding, so annoyingly knowing, that for an instant Lolly wanted to strangle her. She clamped her lips together.

"I know, I know," Carrie soothed. "I've been in love with Colonel Macready for years and years. Women throw themselves at him all the time. Every single time he dances with anyone at a social or a barn dance I die a thousand deaths."

"I am not dying," Lolly murmured. *I just keep thinking about his mouth. Being held in his arms.* She thought it best to change the subject.

"Look, someone is coming out of the gazebo."

Carrie's gaze shot to the enclosure. The curtains parted, and a slightly disheveled Fleurette descended the steps. Hoots and raucous cheers rose from the crowd.

Carrie sighed. "My, doesn't she look like a cat swimming in cream."

Lolly peered at the figure floating toward them. "Cat? Her hair is a bit mussed, but her look has nothing to do with cream."

"What then?" Carrie's soft brown eyes widened in avid interest. "Do you suppose she is stricken with…with…'' She dipped her head to whisper the words. ''Carnal desire?''

Lolly didn't think so, but she'd never felt it, so she couldn't be sure. She'd bet Fleurette's look suggested something else entirely.

''I think she's acting,'' she said carefully.

Carrie gave a little squeak. ''It's my turn now,'' she said as Fleurette settled herself at the opposite end of the iron bench. ''Leora, don't look at my face when I come out. You see everything!''

Lolly pressed her arm and nodded. The young schoolteacher stood up and advanced toward the gazebo with eager steps.

Fleurette did not watch Carrie, Lolly noted. She watched Lolly! When she caught her gaze, the spark of hostility in the green eyes passed instantly into controlled civility. Lolly didn't believe it for one second. Yes, the woman was acting, but why?

Fleurette leaned forward. ''Ah do hope we didn't take too long,'' she purred. She put a slight emphasis on the word *we*.

Lolly wrinkled her nose at the heavy floral scent. ''Why, I scarcely noted the time,'' she lied. ''There is so much to think about in—in these matters.''

Maybe she would try some acting of her own, she decided. ''Compatibility,'' she pronounced clearly. Then, with a careless wave of her hand she added, ''Sexual, of course.''

Fleurette's small, pointed jaw dropped open. "Of course," she echoed in a small voice. "Well, Ah believe the colonel, that is, *Kellen,*" she said with subtle emphasis, "will do admirably in that regard."

Instead of feeling triumphant for having seen through the preening actress, Lolly felt a dart of sadness. In some way she could not explain, she felt sorry for Fleurette.

Sorry for her? The woman was selfish and grasping and everything else Lolly detested, and Lolly felt sorry for her?

Sorry for *what?* The beautiful and accomplished Southern belle was out to snare Colonel Macready, and she was willing to resort to subterfuge to secure her net about him.

A light snapped on in Lolly's head. Why had the word *subterfuge* popped up? All along she'd suspected Fleurette of hiding something. Why else would she, a Southerner, venture so far into Yankee country? Had she perhaps known Colonel Macready before?

Lolly folded her hands in her lap and suppressed the urge to reach into her pocket for her reporter's notepad. All her dresses had pockets, for just that reason.

A cloud of blue pipe smoke descended about her. Mr. Stanton, Lolly surmised without even looking. She recognized the scent. It smelled like Papa's pipe tobacco.

Fleurette made a small show of coughing, and Lolly had to smile. Mr. Stanton stepped forward to offer his handkerchief. Lolly averted her eyes.

Would this evening never end? What was Carrie doing in there so long?

Oh, she knew very well what they were doing. She could scarcely stand the pictures that rose in her imagination.

But she *did* like Carrie Gundersen. She would make a lovely bride.

Then why, she wondered as she unclenched her hands, were fingernail marks etched on her palms?

Chapter Ten

Kellen heard the soft swish of the curtains at the edge of the gazebo. Lord, the ordeal was starting. Quickly he checked his blindfold. Black as night and twice as quiet.

He cocked his ear toward the slight noise a few feet away and stood up. Whoever it was, she'd have to come to him; he couldn't see even a sliver of light beneath the band of soft black velvet Dora Mae had tied over his eyes. Damn the woman. He'd at least like to see who he was kissing.

The rustling came closer. Closer. He opened his mouth to greet her, then remembered they must not speak. Instead, he held out his hand.

Her perfume hit him first, a sweet, flowery scent with a touch of musk rose. Or did he imagine that part? Not having vision, his other senses seemed extra sharp. Maybe Dora Mae knew what she was about after all.

A soft, small hand settled in his. Kellen closed his fingers over it and drew her toward him. Like reeling in a trout.

She was near him now, so near he could hear her light, steady breathing. He moved his hand up her arm, over some soft, insubstantial-feeling fabric through which the warmth of her skin penetrated. He slid his other arm around her waist.

She smelled good. Felt good.

And she would taste…

He bent his head, touched her upturned cheek with his lips and found her mouth. She tasted of apricots. An old trick. She'd gargled with a bit of brandy to sweeten her breath.

He pressed harder, slipped his tongue past her teeth. Still apricots. Nothing but that sweet, sweet taste, but no… No particular jolt of pleasure.

Vaguely disappointed, he continued to move his mouth over hers, going deeper, trying to discover something, though he didn't know exactly what.

Over the years he'd kissed a good many women. It was usually pleasant, sometimes even mildly arousing. Like this one. The experience was provocative in a way; this woman knew what to do with her lips and tongue. She was soft. Willing. But…bland.

When he released her, she clung to him. Raised herself on tiptoe and kissed her way across his face, then blew her breath into his ear.

He liked it. Well enough to kiss her again, which he did. After a long moment he lifted his head. Still bland, goddammit.

Gently he put her aside and turned her toward the curtains.

He felt shaken, but not in an amorous way. His brain yammered at him. *There must be more than this!*

There was a long pause, during which Kellen heard the crowd cheer for some reason, then another swish of the curtain told him the second candidate had entered the gazebo.

An expectant silence fell outside the enclosure as well as inside. Again Kellen reached his hand toward the sound of someone moving near him.

A pair of soft arms wrapped themselves around his waist. Her cheek pressed against his shirtfront, and she hugged him. The scent of violets rose from her hair. Nice. Very nice.

He tipped her chin up with his forefinger and kissed her. Yes, very nice. She drew back slightly when he introduced his tongue, then suddenly opened her mouth under his. It was easy to keep kissing her; she had him pinned at the waist and it was pleasant to just hold on and float.

Eventually she stirred, and he realized he felt no desire to go further. He lifted his lips from hers, heard her sigh, then sigh again. He liked that. Maybe she'd make that sound again if he kissed her some more.

More minutes. More kisses.

More sighs.

But still no desire to go further.

She gave him a final squeeze about the middle and fled. This time his mind split in two; one part stood back and observed himself with sharp eyes. Another part froze in denial.

Let yourself feel, Kellen.

He did. Kissing a woman felt wonderful.

Let yourself want her.

He did that, too. He would enjoy finding either woman in his bed.

Let yourself be swept away, lifted outside yourself. Let it matter.

No. Never again. Oh, God, maybe he'd never be free of Lorena.

Carrie drifted down the gazebo steps, her lips swollen, her eyes glazed.

"How was it, honey?" Fleurette inquired in a syrupy tone.

Carrie's gaze focused slowly. "What?"

"Y'all *did* kiss him, didn't you?"

"What? Oh, yes," she said dreamily. "More than once."

Fleurette gave a little toss of her blond ringlets. "Well?"

Carrie looked so bewitched Lolly had to laugh. The schoolteacher's gaze kept drifting to the gazebo.

"Are you payin' attention? Did you *like* it?"

"Oh, yes indeed," Carrie said on a sigh. "Ever so much."

"Why, yoah completely bedazzled. Just look at her, Leora. Completely bedazzled."

"Oh, yes indeed," Carrie said again. "Ever so much."

Lolly wasn't in the least surprised. Carrie had been "bedazzled" with the colonel long before this evening. She wondered that Fleurette had not noticed.

But she *had* noticed. Right at the beginning, on that first day when all three of them had drunk lemonade together in the hotel dining room. It was Fleurette who'd said Carrie was "obviously smitten with the colonel.'' If she knew this, then why bring it up again?

Because, a wry voice inside her said, *she's poking fun at Carrie's feelings.*

Why would she do such a cruel thing?

Grow up, Lolly. Because Fleurette is desperate. And, she realized suddenly, because Carrie didn't really love the colonel! The schoolteacher was enamored with the *idea* of being in love with him. And Fleurette, being knowledgeable in these matters, knew it.

And of course, Fleurette wants the colonel for herself.

An elbow jostled her ribs. ''Go on,'' Carrie intoned. ''You're next.''

Lolly's bones turned to ice. She couldn't. She couldn't stand up, couldn't face him. Not after making a fool of herself in front of him this afternoon. How could she lose control of her tongue like that whenever he was near?

And then bright sunlight broke through the fog in her brain. *He will be blindfolded.... You are not to speak to each other.*

Bless the Ladies Helpful Society! *He won't know it's me.*

Armored with that knowledge, she climbed the four steps to the gazebo, pushed through the cur-

tains and stepped inside. Kellen Macready stood in
the dim light, a band of black fabric wrapped over
his eyes. Arms folded tight across his midriff, he
looked like a tall, unsmiling military statue cast in
bronze. Well, he *was* a colonel.

But he looked dreadfully stiff and proper. And
completely disinterested. Of course his lips would
be tired by this time. One quick peck, the kind Papa
gave her when she was little, and it would be over.
She drew in a shaky breath and willed some steel
into her spine.

Hesitant, she moved forward, touched his arm to
let him know she was here. Ready for his kiss. Just
as her fingertips brushed his shirtsleeve, he moved.
His arms opened and she stepped forward.

For a long minute he simply held her, as if he
had known she was frightened. As if he had missed
her, had been waiting for her for a long time.

Her breath stopped. She stood motionless within
the circle of his arms, feeling his hard, warm limbs
against her body, knowing on some level deep inside her being that this—being together like this—
had nothing to do with Dora Mae Landsfelter.

Tears stung under her lids. She felt so happy!
Full of light and warmth and yearning such as she
had never known.

Yet at the same time she had never felt so lonely.

She hadn't known *how* lonely until this moment. She never wanted to let go.

She wanted to touch him, his arms, his face. His mouth. She wanted to kiss him and hold him and whisper things she'd held inside all these years.

She lifted her mouth to his.

Kellen lowered his head and found her lips, so warm, so tender, he felt his body tremble. He held her soft, shaking frame and stopped thinking. As he moved his mouth over hers, she drew him into a sweet, dark place where his blood sang with desire and something long buried deep within him clawed to get out.

My God, she was flame and cool water, and he was so thirsty for it. For her. It felt as if he were waking up after a long, long sleep.

Her arms went around his neck, holding him close to her, one hand in his hair, her breasts swelling against his chest.

And then she pulled away. He drew her back, kissed her again and again, first lightly, then deeply. And she answered every unspoken question with her lips and tongue. He could sense the joy in her, the kindling desire. His entire being, body and soul, blood and bone, throbbed with wanting her.

When she stepped away at last, her breathing

uneven, Kellen knew something he wished he didn't.

This woman—whoever she was—could set him afire.

Kellen paced back and forth over the octagonal plank floor of the gazebo, trying to settle his heart-beat into a more normal pace. He'd ripped the blindfold from his eyes and now, facing Dora Mae Landsfelter, he felt like a cornered lion on the plains of Africa. Dora Mae spoke over the noise of the crowd outside.

"Colonel Macready, have you come to a decision?" Her voice seemed to penetrate his pounding brain from far away.

"Colonel Macready?"

"What?"

"A decision," she reiterated. "Have you made one?"

He didn't know how to answer. Did he dare cast his vote for the one woman who had turned his equilibrium upside down? *Did he dare risk getting burned again?*

A glass of Josh Bodwin's applejack might clear his head. Two glasses might let him sleep tonight.

"Colonel? Colonel, please!"

Kellen told her the only thing he could that was

halfway honest. "Now for God's sake tell me who it is so I can stay away from her."

Dora Mae gave him an odd look, bustled to the curtains and drew them back. He looked out on a hundred, maybe two hundred faces gazing up at them in anticipation.

Off to one side, on the iron bench under the maple tree, three well-kissed ladies perched close together, watching Dora Mae in nervous silence. Three feminine concoctions of silk and satin and petticoats and perfume.

He admired all three. But only one of them had turned his heart inside out.

"He's looking at us," Carrie whispered. "Studying each of us like he's going to paint our portraits or something."

"And he's not smilin'." Fleurette twitched her skirt.

"No, but we are," Lolly couldn't resist saying. "We're sitting here like three Rhode Island Reds with our nests full of golden eggs."

"What a vulgar comparison. Weah not doin' anything of the kind."

"Ladies, Dora Mae's about to say something," Lolly said.

"She's going to announce the winner," Carrie

said with a hush in her voice. "There, you see? She's at the podium."

The three women exchanged glances. Suddenly their hands were linked together, and as Dora Mae's mouth opened to speak, three sets of knuckles turned the color of pale marble.

"Ladies and gentlemen, the time has come to announce the winner of this evening's event."

A loud buzzing rippled through the town square, accented by someone yodeling at the top of his lungs. Now *that* was funny.

"Colonel Macready," Dora Mae began. At the mention of his name, the buzzing rose into a crescendo and then faded into expectant quiet.

"Aw, hurry up, Dora Mae," a male voice shouted. "We all need a drink. Prob'ly the colonel needs one most of all!"

Dora Mae gave the man a hard look, but said nothing.

"That was Dora Mae's husband who spoke," Carrie explained in a whisper.

Her husband? A laugh bubbled out of Lolly's throat and she clapped one hand over her mouth. The other was being slowly crushed in Carrie's grip.

Dora Mae stepped up to the podium, the poppies on her hat bobbing. "Colonel Macready has selected…that is, he has expressed a preference for… His vote goes to…'' She paused for dramatic effect so long, Lolly wanted to scream.

"The third and last candidate. Miss Leora Mayfield."

Carrie threw both arms around her. "Leora, that's you! How wonderful that is. Now we're all even."

Two bright spots of color appeared on Fleurette's smooth, white face, but not a word passed her lips. The green eyes flashed in determination and something else Lolly couldn't identify at the moment. She'd seen it before, particularly on that day in the schoolhouse, when she had first met the other two women.

Fear. That was it. Almost…desperation. She'd seen that same look back in Kansas, on the faces of runaway slaves. On her ailing mother's pinched visage when Papa was killed at Chancellorsville.

The crowd began to cheer. Lolly glanced to the gazebo for a look at the colonel, but he had disappeared.

As quickly as she could, Lolly made her excuses and headed toward the hotel. The three candidates had agreed to eat supper together, and right at this moment, she felt she would faint if she didn't put something in her fluttery stomach.

Twenty minutes later, Lolly found herself seated with Fleurette at a cloth-covered table in the hotel dining room. Carrie had stopped to speak with Mrs. Landsfelter after the evening festivities, and would be along shortly.

"It was somethin' about tomorrow," Fleurette explained.

Lolly nodded and studied the menu.

"Don't you want to know *what* about tomorrow?" Fleurette pursued.

Lolly looked straight into the calculating green eyes. "Truly, I do not. I haven't eaten a thing since breakfast, and I'm about to starve. What are you having?"

Fleurette hesitated. "Ah haven't made up mah mind yet." She picked up the leather-backed menu, twisted it sideways, then upside down. "What are *you* having?"

"Steak," Lolly said. "And fried potatoes and gravy. And a big slice of apple pie."

Fleurette's eyes rounded. "All that?"

"All that," Lolly confirmed. "I said I was hungry."

"Well, Ah always try to eat dainty. That's what mah mammy taught me." She fiddled with the menu. "If y'all weren't havin' steak, what would you choose?"

Lolly stared at the young woman, and all at once something clicked in her memory. Yesterday, during the Bramble Scramble, Fleurette had handed over the clue she found at the boat dock. And then Fleurette had asked Lolly to read the note she found tied to the horse's neck. But that made no sense.

Or did it?

Suddenly it was clear. Fleurette might be charming and pretty and gifted and always exquisitely turned out, but... Yes! Lolly was sure of it, now. Fleurette could not read!

"Oh, my dear, I'm so sorr—" She caught herself midsentence. How hard it would be to acknowledge such a deficiency! She took Fleurette's hand.

"If I were tired of steak and potatoes, I'd have, let's see...roast chicken. With snap beans, if they're fresh. Or—" she scanned the menu "—a salad. Coleslaw, maybe. Or Waldorf, with fruit."

Fleurette sent her a look of unspoken gratitude Lolly would never forget. "Thank you, Leora."

That was all she said, but Lolly sensed how much it had cost her. The young woman from New Orleans was two-thirds pride and one-third backbone. She had an inflated sense of herself, but it took a good bit of courage to carry it off.

My, people were such mixtures!

As for herself, Lolly felt a good deal of pride as well. She congratulated herself for having spent twenty-five whole minutes without once thinking of Colonel Kellen Macready.

Mrs. Squires met Kellen at the door, her barely contained curiosity kept in check only because he peeled off his jacket and handed it to her.

"Liked the kissin', did ye, laddie?"

"Why would you think that, Madge?"

"Because ye look half-tottered, and I smell no spirits on your breath. Women can do that to you."

Kellen groaned. Women, no. One woman, yes. Oh, Lord, what had he done?

The housekeeper sped to the coat rack in the wide hallway, hung up his jacket, then marched back to wave her hand in front of his face. "Want some supper?"

"What?"

"Supper! I've some cold chicken and—"

"Whiskey," he interjected. "I'll pour my own, Madge. It was good of you to wait up, but you go on home, now. It's past nine."

"Hummph. It's past ten, laddie. You're not half-awake."

"I'm awake. Just wish I weren't."

The housekeeper eyed him critically. "That bad, is it?"

Kellen could only shrug.

"You mark my words, lad. This is the best thing that could happen to you. You're stuck, that's what you are. Been stuck for the last fifteen years, so you just loosen up and let Dora Mae—"

"Good night, Madge."

"Oh, good night, laddie. You'll forgive an old woman who just wants…"

He bent and kissed her soft, wrinkled cheek. "I'll forgive you anything, you meddlesome female. You know that."

"…babies in the house."

Babies! Good God, he'd almost forgotten how he'd got into this circus in the first place. The Macready heir. Heirs, if Mrs. Squires got her wish.

He couldn't just choose a wife who made him feel good; there would, he hoped, eventually be a child—children—to consider. He needed someone who would be a good companion *and* a good mother.

The thought made him thirsty. When the door closed behind Madge, Kellen headed toward the library, where a full decanter of brandy and an unfinished volume of Poe awaited. Sam lay curled up by his reading chair.

By eleven o'clock he knew no more about Annabel Lee than he had when he started, and he was so restless he felt as if his brain was revolving on a spit.

"Come on, Sam. Let's get women off our minds. Let's go for a midnight ramble."

Chapter Eleven

Drained of all coherent thought, Lolly left the hotel dining room and walked across the street to the town square. It would be deserted now, after Dora Mae's "athletic" event earlier in the evening. She couldn't wait to sink down on the wrought-iron bench and think things out.

She breathed in the warm, still evening air. It smelled of the jasmine that wound up the gazebo walls and arched over the peaked roof. She remembered the scent when the colonel had kissed her.

Lolly closed her eyes and sucked in another deep breath. What a heavenly, sweet perfume. She would never, never forget it. If she stayed in Maple Falls, she would plant jasmine vines along every single fence, just to remind her of this magical night.

If she stayed. Recalling Carrie's words over supper, she realized her position in the town, whether as a married woman or a spinster seeking employment, now depended on her cake-baking skills, for that was to be the next competition.

What she knew about baking cakes she could fit in a thimble. She'd spent her girlhood reading books and writing articles and setting type at the newspaper office. She could compose sentences and correctly spell five-syllable words, better than any other woman in Cherokee County. But bake a cake? Where would she find a recipe? A store? Mixing bowls and cake pans?

Surely her life would not be over if she failed to bake a good cake? Or even failed to marry? Maybe being a thirty-year-old spinster wouldn't be the end of the world, as she had once thought.

A startling new perception was now taking root in her brain, a nagging suspicion about who she really was and what she ought to do about it.

She *liked* Colonel Macready. That had nothing whatsoever to do with her fear of being an old maid; she would like Kellen Macready until the day she died. She hadn't expected to *care* about the man, much less be concerned about whether *he* was happy or not. How callow she had been just four days ago!

Worse, she was becoming genuinely fond of Carrie Gundersen. Even Fleurette LeClair was turning out to be appealing in a roundabout sort of way. Her rivals for Kellen's hand were becoming, well, allies so to speak. What a muddle!

Lolly stared into the shadows shrouding the now uncurtained gazebo and gave a startled gasp. Someone was sitting on the top step! Someone motionless. Silent. He was looking straight at her! She knew that by the white patch in the dark that must be his face.

She gathered her skirt into her left hand and stood up, her muscles tensing. It was only about twenty-five steps from here to the hotel veranda; suddenly it seemed like a thousand miles.

The instant she started off, a long shadow streaked from the gazebo, bounded to her side and began nuzzling her hand. "Sam," she squealed. "Where did you come from?"

"Over here," a low voice responded. "Sorry, Miss Mayfield. My dog thinks you smell good."

Lolly laughed a bit shakily. "I must smell like steak. It's what I ate for supper." She patted Sam's warm head and felt his tail thump against her skirt. When she looked up, Colonel Macready was moving toward her.

"Mind if I sit down?"

''Well, no, I guess not. What were you doing in the gazebo?''

''Nothing. Thinking. I went for a walk with Sam there, and we just kind of ended up here.'' He settled himself at the far end of the bench.

''I see.'' She didn't, really. Why would he be out walking at this hour?

''What are you doing in the park this late?'' he asked.

''Trying to recall a cake recipe.''

He gave a short laugh. ''Anything to do with the Ladies Helpful Society?''

''Well, yes, actually. We're each—Carrie and Fleurette and myself—supposed to make one layer for a stack cake. Many layers, spread with jam and applesauce in between. You know, the kind they serve at wedd—at receptions? It's something to do with the competition.''

''The competition,'' he echoed softly. ''Why am I not surprised? A croquet match, Dora Mae's Bramble Scramble and now a cake-baking marathon. Three more unlikely events I couldn't dream up in a hundred years.''

''You forgot one event.'' Lolly fidgeted with the cuff of her blouse. No force in the universe could get her to utter the word *kiss.*''

"So I did," he breathed. "How do the scores stand now?"

"Fleurette won at croquet. Carrie won the scramble. And I…" There was that word again. She couldn't say it out loud, not to him. Not to the man who had sent her heart tumbling.

"You won this evening's event," he said in a quiet voice. "Hands down, I might add."

"Oh. *Oh.*" Lolly swallowed.

"So the score is tied up at present. How are you at baking cakes?"

"Miserable, I'm afraid."

A look of relief passed over his face. She couldn't be sure, but she thought she saw the glimmer of a smile, but that, too, vanished in an instant.

"Fleurette brought her collection of old family receipts from New Orleans, so I expect she will have no trouble. And Carrie tells me she's been baking cakes since she was eight years old."

Lolly didn't understand why she felt compelled to volunteer this information, but it seemed to make the colonel perk up, so she was glad she did. She also didn't understand why, as his spirits apparently rose, hers plummeted. She plunked down on the opposite end of the bench as the wind whooshed out of her.

The colonel goes up, I go down. Like a teeter-totter.

And right then, at that very moment, she knew how it would end.

As quickly as she had sat down, she popped up again.

He caught her hand and tugged her down once more. Very gingerly she scrunched herself tight into the farthest space from him.

"You are very generous to your rivals, Miss Gundersen and Miss LeClair."

"They may be rivals, but they're not my enemies. I mean, I didn't know them at first, but we've been talking things over and, well, Carrie is a dear, really. She means no harm to anyone, and Fleurette—well, I think she can be very sweet when she wants to be."

"One would almost think you wished for one of them, your rivals, to win."

"Oh, my, no," she blurted. "In the worst way I want to…well, I'll be thirty in another month and I had hoped…"

Oh, Lord, could she never keep her mouth shut around this man?

"I came to Maple Falls to marry, Colonel. To marry you, as a matter of fact. And then things turned out to be more complicated than I had thought.''

"Did they, indeed?'' He sounded amused.

"Yes. Much more complicated.'' If he only knew how complicated.

"And now?''

"Well, it does seem funny, but when I arrived I didn't know you at all, and I was desperate to marry you. Now I do know you, somewhat, that is. And I am no longer desperate.''

"That's not very flattering. You mean that I have not measured up to your expectations?''

"Oh, no. I like you! I really do. You measure up just wonderfully. *More* than wonderfully.''

He went absolutely still, but she could hear the change in his breathing.

"It's the oddest thing,'' she continued, watching his face. "I want to be happy, it's true. But now I also want *you* to be happy. That's why I'm not desperate any more. You must make the right choice for *you,* don't you think?''

Kellen swallowed over a lump the size of a hard-boiled egg. He wished she hadn't said that. Wished she wasn't so open. So earnest. Something about her transparent honesty cut a big fat hole in his heart and made him acutely aware of the hunger he'd kept hidden from himself for so many years.

He wished he could dislike her. Find something about her that didn't make him smile inside, or feel that frightening rush of warmth under his breastbone. God help him, he wished he didn't want her in the way a man wants a woman.

"Miss Mayfield?"

"Yes, Colonel Macready?"

"Miss Mayfield. Leora. You are one in a million."

Kellen stood up, drew himself to attention and snapped her a military salute.

That and more. He wished he'd never laid eyes on her.

"Mr. Bodwin, I need a kitchen."

The mercantile owner's eyebrows shot upward. "You want a house around it, like most folks?"

"Just the kitchen. You see, I have to bake a cake for the—"

"Bride competition," he supplied. "Yep, I know all about that. Whole town's workin' up an appetite."

"Mr. Bodwin…"

"You any better at baking than y'are at croquet?" He studied her face for a long minute. "Oh. Sorry I asked. Still and all, you came to the right place."

A faint glimmer of hope penetrated the cloud of gloom Lolly had carried with her into the mercantile. "You know how to bake cakes?"

"Naw. But I do know of a kitchen you could use for a day. Mrs. Squires, over on Peach Street. It's not exactly *her* kitchen, but she rules the roost, so to speak."

"Mrs. Squires... The name sounds familiar. Isn't she...?"

"Yep. Colonel Macready's housekeeper. Marjorie, her name is."

"But..."

"Me an' Evalee—that's my wife—we've known Mrs. Squires a good long while. Evalee and her stitch quilts together every Thursday afternoon, and our oldest girl married one of the Squires boys."

"But..."

"No 'buts,' now. This here's a nice, friendly town. Folks like to help out. Come to think of it, that's how come we got a Ladies Helpful Society in the first place."

Lolly closed her lips. In her opinion, the Ladies Helpful Society was both a blessing and a curse. However, Joshua Bodwin, the dear man, was the answer to a rattled spinster's prayers.

But the colonel's own kitchen?

Well, why not? Carrie had a kitchen to work in.

Even Fleurette, who was boarding with Mrs. Petrov, had access to the kitchen. Lolly couldn't ask to use the hotel kitchen, even though the proprietor had been very kind and thoughtful from her very first day in Maple Falls. Mrs. Squires was her only hope.

"Is there a time when…I mean, when the colonel won't be at home?"

"Dunno about that, Miss Leora. You just go on over and tap at the back door for Mrs. S. Tell her Josh Bodwin sent you."

Lolly groaned inside. The phrase "between a rock and a hard place" didn't do justice to the way she felt at this moment. Between a hot stove and a cold bed was more like it.

Oh, bother Dora Mae Landsfelter anyway. Lolly had half a notion to pack up her things and take the first train back to Kansas.

But she couldn't. Not now. She might have managed it the day before, before she and Colonel Macready had engaged in their "athletic pursuit," as Fleurette termed it. But not today. Today she knew more, felt more, *cared* more about the mysteries between a man and a woman than she had ever dreamed of. She could not leave.

Besides, she reminded herself, she knew for sure how this would all turn out.

"Thank you, Mr. Bodwin. Once again I am in your debt."

"You just save me a piece of that stacked-up creation you ladies are bakin'."

The following afternoon, armed with *Mrs. Beeton's Receipts* checked out of the Maple Falls library, Lolly trudged up the hill to Colonel Macready's residence on Peach Street.

It really was a lovely house, with gingerbread wood trim and tall windows, even a rounded turret on one corner. Any woman in her right mind would admire it. Shade trees marked the front walkway, and the path that led past the elegant three-story structure was bordered with crimson dahlias and drifts of rose-pink nicotiana. Purple wisteria enveloped the grape arbor next to the carriage house, and, oh my, wouldn't Fleurette love that! A pond in the lattice-screened side yard, complete with a fountain spouting water from a young boy's...

My heavens! How suggestive. Even Fleurette would blush at that. Lolly didn't stop grinning until she reached the back porch steps.

At her first hesitant tap, the door swung open.

"Mrs. Squires? I am—"

"Yes, yes, come in, lass." The woman enveloped Lolly in a bosomy hug, then held her at arm's length. "Ah, yes, just as I thought." The house-keeper gave her shoulders a hefty squeeze and bustled away into the kitchen.

"Come in, come in! The hens just laid six fine eggs for your undertaking. I'll just chunk up my fire while you put on an apron, over there on the peg."

The apron, blue gingham with ruffles around the edge, hung to Lolly's calves and the flounce at the neck tickled her chin. Mrs. Squires was even taller than Lolly.

The housekeeper took one look and let out a yelp of laughter. "With your blue eyes and that cover-up, lass, ye look like a great tall hollyhock!"

Lolly wondered if that was a compliment. "The question is, can this hollyhock make a cake?"

The housekeeper yelped again. "Course ye can. Whyever not?"

Lolly hesitated. She hated to admit her inexperience in the kitchen, but she hated even more the idea of fibbing to the older woman who had agreed to help her.

"Mrs. Squires, can you keep a secret?"

"Depends," the woman said shortly.

Lolly blinked. "On what?"

The housekeeper met her gaze with unflinching directness. "On whether it helps Colonel Macready or hurts him. I'll protect that boy with my life if it comes down to it.''

That was good enough for Lolly. The woman was obviously devoted to the colonel.

''Mrs. Squires, I cannot cook. Nor can I bake or keep house. I would make a rather...inefficient wife for Colonel Macready.''

The housekeeper tilted her head and studied Lolly. ''I hear croquet isn't among your skills, either.''

''No, I'm afraid not.''

''I see.''

Lolly sighed. ''I am accomplished as a *person,* though not necessarily as a woman. I've spent many years on my own, working hard at my writing and the newspaper I owned, but...''

''Do ye read much?'' the housekeeper inquired, her face stony.

''Yes, I'm afraid I do.''

''Prefer bein' alone to tea party chatter?''

''Y-yes.'' The bubble of hope she'd nurtured began to deflate.

Mrs. Squires flashed a grin at her. ''You'll do, lass! You'll do.'' She pointed to the round oak kitchen table.

''Sit yourself down, my girl. Study your receipts,

and we'll pick out a lollapaloozer. And ye'll have some tea, won't you?''

Lolly stirred the batter with a wooden spoon, then beat the mixture until her arm ached. Five hundred strokes, Mrs. Squires recommended. With all the melted chocolate and walnuts, the mixture was so thick it was like mud pudding. She'd just add a splash more of the Jamaican rum.

She counted the five hundred strokes, poured the batter into the large square pan she had selected from Mrs. Squires's utensil collection and slid it into the hot oven. Now, in just three-quarters of an hour, her masterpiece would be ready.

The housekeeper had sped off somewhere, so Lolly turned the hourglass over and settled down at the table to wait. She sipped the fresh cup of tea Mrs. Squires had brewed, thumbed through Mrs. Beeton's Receipts, and watched the sand trickle away the minutes.

Footsteps thumped in the hallway outside. Mrs. Squires returning to check on her, no doubt. But it was not the housekeeper's voice that brought Lolly bolt upright.

''What the hell are you doing here?'' Colonel Macready loomed in the doorway, his tall frame tensed, hands clenched into fists.

"I'm baking a cake!"

"I don't mean what are you *doing,* I mean why *here?* In my house?" His voice was low and rumbly but it shook just the tiniest bit.

Lolly bristled. "What difference does it make? All I'm using is the oven and a few bowls and a cake pan."

He paced past the black iron stove to the back door, then retraced his steps to the door into the dining room. Two more circuits, and then he halted in front of her.

"I think we should not be alone together."

Lolly's first reaction was to go liquid inside, like cocoa and rum heated over a fire. Her second reaction was to feel the prick of hot anger.

"I was here first!"

"No, you weren't. This is *my* house."

"I mean today. You didn't need to charge into the kitchen as if you owned it."

"I do own it."

"You know what I mean," Lolly snapped.

"I do, indeed. Unfortunately."

"I am invading your privacy, is that it?"

Kellen flinched. "Something like that." His privacy. His refuge. His heart. The heart he'd protected with such care all these years. He risked a look at her clear blue eyes, now heated to violet in anger. *Dear God, how he wanted her.*

"Miss Mayfield?"

"Yes, Colonel Macready?" Her voice was crisp with alarm.

"Please leave my kitchen." He said the words so softly he wasn't sure she would hear.

"No. I won't. I can't, not until my cake is done."

"And don't come back." He finished issuing his order and cringed at how his voice sounded, exactly like an army officer ordering troops to battle. God help him, she was destroying what little equilibrium he'd salvaged after the war.

"When I leave," she shot back, "which will not be for another —" she glanced at the hourglass "—ten minutes, I will not come back. Never. I will never set foot in this house again, I promise you."

Kellen stared at her for a full minute. She was magnificent. A lioness defending her lair.

Except that it was *his* lair.

And it was his hand that wanted to touch her trembling chin, his body that hungered to feel her passion. Her fire.

"Goddammit, Leora."

"Goddammit what?" She spit the words at him, and all at once he couldn't stand it one more second. He caught her in his arms and held her until she stopped struggling, and then he kissed her.

Big, big tactical error. Her lips under his were like warm velvet. Suddenly he wanted his mouth, and his hands, on every inch of her skin.

"Stop," she said after a few exquisitely sensual explorations of her neck and throat. "Kellen, you must stop."

"Why must I?" he murmured against her hair.

"Because…"

"Because?" He kissed her again. Might as well be hung for a lioness as for a lamb. This time when his tongue touched her lips, it was like hot wine pouring into his blood; he didn't want to stop. Ever.

"Because," she moaned against his mouth. "I think…"

"You think what?" he whispered.

"I think my cake is done."

Chapter Twelve

"Aren't they just luscious looking?" Carrie folded her small, capable hands under her chin and gazed admiringly at the three square cake layers on her kitchen table.

"Ah think mine should go on top, don't y'all?" Fleurette touched one finger to the tender white layer she had turned out on one of Carrie's dinner plates. "It's mah great-grandmother's silver almond cake."

Lolly wondered suddenly how she had managed to read her great-grandmother's recipe, but she stopped herself from asking. It would embarrass Fleurette and, worse, reveal her secret to Carrie. Or perhaps she carried the recipe in her memory.

A thoughtful Carrie laid a finger on her chin. "Mine is a spice cake made with molasses. And

Leora's is chocolate. You're quite right, Fleurette. Your layer should go on top.''

"Course Ah am," Fleurette said complacently. "Chocolate is so…well, heavy.''

Lolly gaped at the young woman. Of course it was heavy. *Her* layer was chock-full of things a man was supposed to like—chocolate, walnuts, even rum. With all Fleurette's knowledge of the opposite sex, why hadn't she thought of that?

"How will we stack up the layers? What will hold them together?'' Lolly ventured.

"Toothpicks," Fleurette said.

"Applesauce," Carrie countered. "At least that's how my mother does it. "Like a filling.''

"Then hadn't we better peel some apples?'' Lolly looked around for an apron.

"We could use preserves instead," Fleurette suggested.

"Don't want to get your hands dirty, is that it?'' Carrie softened her words by squeezing Fleurette's slim shoulders.

"Why, no, that's not it at all,'' Fleurette protested. "Just that it's quicker.''

"I've already made the applesauce," Carrie said. "Last night, after supper. There's a big bowl of it chilling in the cooler.''

They slathered on applesauce, piled the layers

on top of one another and then all three stepped back to admire the effect. Lolly thought the cake looked like the base of an Egyptian temple. The final layer, Fleurette's white almond cake, slightly smaller than the others, floated on its bed of applesauce like Cleopatra's royal barge.

"Now for the frosting," Carrie said. "What about my aunt Dortha's Demerara sugar icing? And let's put something on top," she added. "A bride, made out of frosting!"

"Or a flower?" Lolly suggested. "A yellow rose, maybe. And yellow nasturtiums around the edge."

"A flag!" Fleurette chirped. "A bonnie blue flag." Wide-eyed, she met the looks Carrie and Lolly sent her.

"Oh, Ah s'pose not."

Once again Lolly found herself puzzling over why a young woman from the South would come north, to Yankee country, to marry. It didn't make sense.

Two hours later, at seven in the evening, Carrie slid their exquisitely frosted triple-layer creation onto the square milk glass cake plate that she retrieved from her hope chest. Then all three of the women untied their aprons, tidied their hair and set off for what Lolly termed The Viewing, at the Golden Valley Hotel.

By the time they arrived, a sizable crowd had gathered.

"Oh, look," Fleurette breathed as they ascended the bright red steps. "Theah's all sorts of people waitin' for us."

"Hungry people," Carrie added. "Dora Mae says everybody in town wants a taste of our cake."

Fleurette tossed her golden ringlets. "Dora Mae told *me* that seven particular gentlemen would be served first."

"Did Dora Mae say *which* particular gentlemen?" Lolly studied the young woman. She wore pale peach silk this evening, and her cheeks had two high spots of color. It couldn't be rouge; no proper young lady would dare to use any sort of face paint. Excitement, probably. By the end of this evening, one of them would be elected to marry Colonel Macready.

An odd, hollow feeling bloomed in the pit of Lolly's stomach. *Oh, please, let it be me.*

"The only one particular gentleman's name Ah remember is Colonel Macready. Oh, and Mr. Stanton, that railroad man. The others just plain slip mah mind."

"Mr. Hickmeyer," Carrie said. "And the mayor,

Mr. Bowman, and Josh Bodwin. Oh, and Eli Shu-maker. He owns the Valley Bank.''

"That's only six gentlemen," Lolly said quietly.

Carrie looked startled. "Oh. And Orven Tillot-sen. The newspaper editor.''

Fleurette's dainty hand flew to her throat. "And all seven will be tastin' our cake?''

"All seven. After that, Dora Mae's cutting pieces for the crowd.''

"And counting the votes from the seven gentle-men," Lolly added.

Carrie set the cake plate down on the center table where Dora Mae and the other two Helpful Ladies waited, cake servers in hand.

"Mathematically, that means there can't be a tie," Carrie whispered. "And of course the men don't know which of us baked what layer.''

Lolly started. What if Colonel Macready didn't *like* chocolate?

Ruth Underwood sat at a nearby table collecting money in the donation jar. A two-bit piece entitled a person to one slice of cake after the jury had voted. Dora Mae waved at the three women, raised a silver knife and tapped for silence.

"Gentlemen of the jury, shall we begin?" Dora Mae cut a small slice from each of the three layers, assembled them on a plate that Minnie Sullivan delivered to Colonel Macready and the other six men who sat together at a large round table in the corner.

The onlookers grew quiet. Minnie fluttered back and forth until all seven had been served, and then Dora Mae gave the signal and seven forks rose to the task at hand.

Lolly, Carrie and Fleurette instinctively moved to a table in the opposite corner, where they huddled together, watching the men's mouths open, close, and chew.

Fleurette clasped her hands on top of the tablecloth. "Ah cain't stand the suspense!"

Lolly and Fleurette watched, mesmerized, as the gentlemen consumed their cake. At one point, Sol Stanton groaned in obvious pleasure, and Fleurette stiffened.

"Ah believe that's mah layer he's eatin'," she whispered. "Oh, Ah just cain't look." She averted her eyes to study her interlaced fingers. "Is he smilin'?"

"Is who smiling?" Lolly murmured. "They're all smiling. And still eating."

Kellen's first bite held a delicious surprise. Featherlight, a whiff of almonds and icing that melted in his mouth.

"An angel baked this," Sol remarked, laying down his fork. "You ever taste anything so fine?"

Orven Tillotsen swallowed audibly. "Middle layer's mighty good, too." He closed his lips over another forkful.

"Naw," Sol said. "The top layer is delicate. Refined. Like a lady's secrets."

"Hell, Sol, it's a cake, not a petticoat."

"Poetry, Orv. I can see the woman behind this creation. Soft and tender as moonlit snow."

The mayor and the banker, Eli Shumaker, chewed away saying nothing.

Kellen sampled the middle layer. Sugar and spice. Old-fashioned. He wondered if Sol was right; could he envision the woman who'd baked this cinnamon and nutmeg wonder?

"Second layer's a bit more...straightforward, would you say, Sol?"

Sol licked icing off his lips. "Spirited. Flavorful. But no poetry."

Josh Bodwin stabbed his fork into the spice layer for the third time. "Just floats around on your tongue and sings its way down your throat. Lord, I wish Evalee could bake like this. She makes good stew, though."

The other men said nothing, just munched away

in silence. Kellen finished the second layer and raised his fork over the dark, fine-textured cake on the bottom.

Lolly reached to pat Fleurette's clenched hands. "Fleurette, calm down. It's not a matter of life and death."

"Oh, but it is!" Fleurette blurted. "Ah cain't go back to N'Awlins now that…"

A zing of curiosity darted into Lolly's brain. "Now that what?" she prompted. Out of the corner of her eye she saw Carrie heading toward them, a tall glass of lemonade in each hand. Behind her trailed Hank Morehouse with the third glass.

"Now that what?" Lolly repeated.

For just an instant, Fleurette's green eyes looked directly into Lolly's. "I…"

"Yes?" Lolly thought she would pop as the silence stretched and Carrie and Hank drew closer.

"I…" The young woman swallowed, glanced sideways at the table of seven men, swallowed again. "You mustn't tell a soul, Leora. Ah couldn't bear it. Promise?"

Her voice was just unsteady enough to warn Lolly. Whatever it was, it was very, *very* important to Fleurette. She gazed at the young woman's rose-spotted cheeks. Maybe it *was* a matter of life and death.

"I promise," Lolly said gently.

"Well, then..." Fleurette drew in a shaky breath. "Ah am expectin.'

Lolly blinked. "Expecting what?"

Fleurette's eyes filled with tears. "Oh, mah gracious sakes, cain't y'all guess?"

"You don't mean a—?" She couldn't bring herself to utter the word *baby*.

A glass of lemonade plunked down in front of her. "Why, you two look like the world's come to an end," Carrie sang. "Here, have some lemonade."

Across the table, Lolly and Fleurette surveyed each other. So *that* was why she had come north. Oh, the poor woman. How hard it must have been. How alone she must feel, and how awfully frightened.

Yes, for Fleurette, it most certainly *was* life and death.

Lolly reached across the table and laid her hand over Fleurette's.

Kellen closed his eyes and let the rich chocolatey flavor tease the inside of his mouth. Good God, he tasted rum! And nuts. Walnuts, if he wasn't mistaken. He let the flavors meld while his tongue explored the texture. Rich. Passionate, even.

"Gentlemen," he announced, his voice choked, "if an angel made the top layer, a devil made this one."

Sol stopped eating. "Yeah?"

"Yeah. I've never tasted anything like it in my life. It's almost…" He hesitated over the word that came to mind.

Sol's bushy eyebrows quivered. "Yeah? Almost what, Kell?"

"Erotic."

Six forks zeroed in on the chocolate layer on their plates.

"Food of the gods," Orv groaned when he could speak. "*All* the gods."

"I've died and gone to heaven," Eli Shumaker said. He forked up another mouthful. "If you don't mind, I'm going to stay here a while."

Tears rose in Sol's eyes. "What a woman!"

"Better than the first?" Kellen inquired.

"Nope. That one's pure angel."

Orven shoveled in a final bite of the chocolate layer. "This one is pretty damn down-to-earth." He blushed, which made all the men chuckle.

"Feet on the ground. Stirring arm in the clouds," Sol sighed. "I'd never let this one out of the kitchen."

Josh smacked his lips. "I'd never let her out of the bedroom!"

Kellen thought exactly the same thing. He lifted his fork again.

Two fat teardrops rolled unchecked down Fleurette's cheeks.

"Are you watching?" Carrie whispered. "Colonel Macready is almost finished, and he's frowning something fierce."

"Is he?" Lolly tried to sound interested. Her chest squeezed painfully at the expression on Fleurette's face. She had to keep Carrie's attention focused elsewhere for the moment.

"What is happening with the other men?" She nudged Fleurette's lemonade glass closer to the woman's clenched hands and took a long drink of her own. More fervently than ever she wished it was Josh Bodwin's applejack instead of lemonade. Perhaps if she took her glass next door to the barroom, Charlie could add some strong spirits. Oh, God, she wished she knew what to say to Fleurette. What to *do*.

Carrie gave a little squeak. "They're all talking now. About the cake, I guess. Mr. Shumaker is waving his fork, and…well I'll be…"

Lolly forced her gaze from Fleurette to the

men's table. Orven Tillotsen was on his feet, leaning toward Sol Stanton in a threatening way. Colonel Macready thrust one hand between them, and abruptly Orven resumed his seat. Josh Bodwin and Mayor Bowman glared at each other across their empty plates.

Colonel Macready signaled Dora Mae to serve up the remainder of the cake, and while the crowd jostled into a ragged line, Ruth Underwood slipped the seven men pencils and small squares of paper.

"They are voting!" Carrie breathed. She gulped down three big swallows of her lemonade. "My nerves aren't a bit calm," she announced.

"Nor are mine." Fleurette's voice sounded perfectly normal. Lolly silently commended the young woman's stage presence.

"I'm nervous as a grasshopper," Lolly admitted.

"Ah feel like mah heart's about to fly right out of mah bosom."

Carrie sighed. "I'm… You know, it's funny, but right now I feel kind of, well, neutral."

"Neutral!" two voices cried.

"Ah thought y'all had singular feelin's for Colonel Macready?"

"Well, I do," Carrie admitted. "I always have, ever since I was seven years old. I'd marry him in a minute if I win the competition. But somehow I feel…"

"Carrie, what do you mean, 'neutral'?" Lolly stared at the schoolteacher's earnest, round face and soft brown eyes and felt her understanding of her own sex crumble. How could a woman feel neutral about a man she'd been in love with for years? Or even *thought* she'd been in love with?

She caught Hank Morehouse's eye and waved him over.

"Take this glass to the barkeep next door," she whispered in his ear. "Ask him to add some…" She whispered the rest of her instructions and slipped a dollar bill into Hank's palm.

Hank nodded at her instructions. Just as he started to turn away, Fleurette pushed her own glass forward. Without a word, Hank picked it up, as well, then eyed Carrie's glass with a questioning look.

But the schoolteacher's attention was glued to the seven slips of paper, now folded and dropped, one by one, into the china saucer in Ruth Underwood's hand.

The votes were in.

Lolly stared at the ballot-covered saucer until her eyes burned. Thank the Lord, it would be over soon. She was so mixed-up inside she fancied she heard church bells tolling in her ears.

Carrie was neutral? And Fleurette wasn't acting now. The young woman was desperate, really desperate.

Lolly wanted to help her, ease her distress if she could, but her mind thunked to a standstill when she tried to puzzle out *how* to help. She squirmed on the hard chair, felt her petticoat bunch up into a knot of limp cotton under her knees.

Hank returned with the two doctored lemonades just as the Helpful Ladies convened two tables away to count the ballots.

The first indication that something was wrong occurred when Minnie Sullivan's hands fell, motionless, into her lap. Lolly stopped breathing.

"What is it?" Carrie whispered.

A fusillade of elderly female voices erupted over the murmuring in the crowded dining room. The flowers on Dora Mae's hat trembled. "That is not possible," she pronounced. She spoke so loudly everyone in the dining room could hear her.

"It *is* possible." Ruth Underwood shoved a slip of white paper across the table. "Look here, Dora. It's plain as oatmeal."

Dora Mae snatched up the paper and gave a piteous-sounding moan. Minnie's hand reappeared and gathered up the remaining ballots with little fluttery motions. "Let's count them, just to be sure."

"Agreed." Ruth poised her pencil above a lined note tablet. Dora Mae's head remained bowed as Minnie unfolded the individual slips of paper, one by one.

"One vote for the almond layer," Minnie read out. Ruth made a mark on her tablet. Minnie Sullivan stowed the voting slip in an empty teacup.

"One vote for the middle layer, the spice one. One for the chocolate layer on the bottom…" Her voice droned on and the room grew increasingly quiet.

When the Helpful Ladies finished counting, Ruth touched Dora Mae's arm.

Dora Mae raised her head. "What is the final tally?"

"Two, two and two. A tie."

Carrie turned a white face toward Lolly. "A tie!" she murmured. "Dora Mae will have a conniption fit."

"Ah'm already havin' one." Fleurette fanned herself with her napkin and took a healthy swig of her lemonade.

"But there are seven men," Lolly whispered. "Seven ballots. How can it be a tie?"

Carrie jerked to a standing position, craning her neck to see the papers in Minnie's teacup. She sat down just as suddenly. "The last ballot was turned in with a question mark."

"A question mark!" Lolly and Fleurette said in one breath. All three women swiveled toward the gentlemen's table.

Which one of those faces looked undecided? Lolly studied each man and finally gave up with a sigh. Poker faces, all seven of them. Even the ones with chocolate on their chins.

A flushed Dora Mae rose and rapped her knife against the cake plate. "The final count," she announced to the onlookers in a trembly voice, "is a tie. Two votes for each layer and one, um, abstention."

The crowd greeted this with jubilation. When the roar died down, Dora Mae continued. "Mrs. Underwood and Mrs. Sullivan will now serve portions of the cake. Following that, the Ladies Helpful Society will immediately convene on the veranda for an emergency meeting." The elderly woman sank onto her chair and handed the silver cake server to Minnie.

Laughter broke out among the seven men serving as judges. Sol's pipe smoke puffed into a blue cloud over the table. "Well, gents, this is one for the books."

"And the newspaper," Orven added.

"Who the hell…?" The men stared at one another, but no one owned up to the question mark.

"Makes sense in a way," Josh Bodwin said at last. "Kinda smart strategy. A tie will make 'em go one more round."

"More to watch," Orven said with undisguised relish. "More contributions for Dora Mae's school fund. And it's great newspaper copy! Gettin' more interesting all the time."

Kellen was the only one who didn't smile.

The three bride candidates bent their heads together over their lemonade glasses. "What happens now?" Carrie asked.

Fleurette downed a big gulp of her doctored lemonade.

"I think," Lolly began when she'd had a double swallow from her own glass, "that *we* should decide what happens next."

"And the colonel," Fleurette said quickly. "Surely he ought to have a say in the matter?"

Carrie peered across the room. "I'm afraid the Ladies Helpful Society got to him first. He's going out on the veranda with Minnie and Dora Mae."

"Mah Great-Aunt Nellie's knickers, do something, Leora!"

"Do what?" Lolly said in a reasonable tone. "Let Colonel Macready handle Dora Mae. He'll take the starch out of her, and then—"

"We-all will decide."

"Decide on what?" Carrie said suspiciously.

Lolly understood in a flash. "On the tie-breaker, of course. We'll think up the next competitive event. The *final* event."

Fleurette nodded emphatically. "Ah agree with Leora."

Carrie groaned aloud. "Seventy-five percent of me agrees, too. The other twenty-five percent doesn't want to think about it any more tonight."

Lolly and Fleurette exchanged glances over their almost empty glasses of lemonade. "Seems lak this marryin' business takes longer than Ah evah thought."

"It won't take more than another few days to settle it. Especially," Lolly added with emphasis, "if we stick together."

Carrie nodded her assent. "All for one and may the best bride win. Are we still agreed?"

"Ah'm willin'. Y'all have been…nice to me."

Lolly swallowed the last of her lemonade over a throat that suddenly ached.

Chapter Thirteen

"A whole evenin'? Alone with the colonel? At his residence?" Fleurette's green eyes widened in delight.

Lolly couldn't believe Dora Mae had accepted their suggestion.

"Naturally you will be chaperoned," Dora Mae offered. "Mrs. Squires, the colonel's housekeeper, and one of the Helpful Ladies will be on the premises, as well."

Carrie plucked at the sleeve of Dora Mae's sky-blue pongee day dress. "What are we supposed to do during that evening?"

"Why, entertain the man, of course!" Dora Mae commanded. "Spend a pleasant evening 'at home' together, so to speak."

Fleurette's rigid spine visibly softened. "Y'all

mean be a charmin' female companion.'' She sent Dora Mae a dazzling smile.

Carrie sniffed. ''What's an evening in the colonel's company going to prove? I would have thought the Ladies Helpful Society would come up with something more challenging.''

To Lolly, this was plenty challenging. So challenging that her mind whirled into a fizz of terror and indecision at the prospect.

''The Ladies Helpful Society didn't come up with this,'' Dora Mae protested. ''The colonel did.''

A groan of despair built inside Lolly. She could never compete with Fleurette, so lovely and so experienced in social niceties. And other things, she thought darkly. Athletic things.

Neither could she compete with Carrie, who was quick and intelligent and so likable no one could resist her. And both of them young and...well, slim as water reeds.

''How long will the entertainment evening last?'' she inquired.

''From seven until ten o'clock. The colonel suggested you draw lots to see who comes on which evening.''

Lolly felt sick. Three hours to fill. Three whole hours and not one rational, entertaining thought in her head. Carrie would propose some sort of game—checkers, perhaps. Or chess or gin rummy. She'd heard the colonel played cards every Wednesday night.

And Fleurette would seduce him, plain and simple. She knew all the feminine tricks, and in her present predicament she needed to win, no matter what.

And Lolly would…well, she would come up with something.

Dora Mae proffered three matchsticks, their lengths hidden in her curled-up fist. Fleurette drew first. Carrie drew the longest stick. Again, Lolly drew the short straw. She would entertain the colonel last, after both Carrie and Fleurette impressed him. By then, the man would be entertained out of his wildest dreams or completely fuddled. Maybe both.

Not only that, the last time she'd entered Colonel Macready's house, she'd sworn never again to set foot in it.

"Ye needn't be so jittery, laddie." Mrs. Squires stepped back to inspect the silk knot she had tied at Kellen's neck. "Ye've known Miss Careen most of her life. 'Tisn't like she's a stranger."

"I've known Careen as a child, Madge. And when she grew up, as a teacher. Not as a woman."

"To be courted," the housekeeper added. "Faith, Kellen, it won't take much—the girl's been daft over you for years."

"Puppy love."

"She doesn't think so. She'll want to darn your socks and fix your tea and give you sons."

Kellen gritted his teeth. "I can't go through with this, Madge."

"Then don't." She sent him a sly look. "Turn the girl out and stay a bachelor till you're ninety-three, like old Tom Gilberti. You can keep each other company on cold winter nights."

"Madge…"

"There's the bell. Good luck, laddie."

It turned out to be one of the longest evenings Kellen could remember. More than merely tedious, it was nerve-racking, like waiting in his tent for the weather to clear so he could move his troops forward.

He and Careen played tiddledywinks until his thumb ached. She never grew tired; her interest in the game never flagged. She was diligent and thorough and she never gave up. Admirable qualities in a woman. Superlative qualities for a mother.

But at the prospect of more evenings like this

one, year after year, Kellen admitted the truth to himself. He was bored. Being with sincere, open, uncomplicated Careen was just a tad on the dull side.

But that's exactly what you wanted. Peace and quiet. No sparks. No anguish.

Yeah, that's what I wanted, all right. He hadn't considered what it would actually be like if he *got* what he wanted.

At precisely ten o'clock, Kellen walked Careen to the front porch, where he had a buggy waiting to drive her home. At the door she turned and looked up at him with adoration in her eyes.

"Oh, Colonel, I've dreamed of an evening like this with you since I was a little girl. I hope it pleased you as much as it did me."

Kellen took her hands in his. "Careen, you are a lovely young woman. Any man would be honored to have you as a partner. But…"

Her soulful brown eyes widened. "But?"

"Well, um, I'm…too old for you."

"You're not! I calculated it out. You're only forty-three. You have lots of years left!"

That, Kellen thought, was the problem in a walnut shell. He had no desire to be close to Careen, to touch her or kiss her, or anything else, whether for five minutes or twenty years. Oh, Lord, he knew he couldn't face a future of tiddledywinks.

Gently he cupped her chin and brushed his lips across her mouth, then rested them against her forehead. "Thank you for coming, Careen."

He handed her into the buggy, signaled to the driver and watched the round yellow wheels carry her away down the hill. The minute he closed the front door he headed to the library and the brandy decanter.

For the third time in as many minutes, Kellen edged to the far end of the maple settee in his parlor. Miss LeClair looked up at him through bronzy eyelashes, gave him a dimpled smile and hitched herself closer. Then she glided across the room and slid closed the pocket door into the dining room, where Mrs. Squires and Ruth Underwood sat drinking tea and serving as chaperones.

"The fireplace heats that room," Kellen remarked. "I leave the door open because it gets chilly in there."

"Why, Colonel, Ah do declare. It is a very warm evenin', like summertime down in N'Awlins. Surely no one could take a chill on a night like this." She settled close to him once more.

"Mrs. Squires is an older woman. Scottish."

"Theah, you see? She's used to bein' cold."

Kellen rose and reopened the door, as much to protect himself as to share the warm air. The instant he resumed his seat, Miss LeClair inched nearer on the pretext of sharing a crystal dish of chocolate drops. "Mah, but these are so rich and sweet. Do have some, Colonel?"

She ran her small, pointed tongue over her upper lip and popped a candy past her teeth, watching him with unsettlingly hungry green eyes.

She was attractive, Kellen had to admit. Quite beautiful, in fact. Delicate and dainty as a breath of spring in that diaphanous mint-green concoction. The lilt and drawl of her speech made him suddenly homesick for the South. For the Virginia plantation he'd inherited from his father and left because he couldn't stand being there. Not after Lorena. He'd sold the land and come to Oregon to lick his wounds.

He closed his eyes, forced himself to breathe in Miss LeClair's perfume. Lilac and gardenia with a heavy, musky undertone. When he opened his lids, she had drawn closer still.

He raised the candy dish between them. "Miss LeClair, are you fond of chocolate?"

"Ah am fond of many things, Colonel." Her

voice dropped to a suggestive whisper. "*Many* things." She swayed toward him.

Good God. Suddenly it occurred to him what the woman's real intent might be. He'd better keep her talking.

"Such as?" he prompted.

"Crayfish," she replied instantly. "And tatting. Ah make extremely fine lace edgings. Then there's music. Ah am most partial to Schubert."

He seized on Schubert. "Perhaps you would play for me?" He gestured to the Erard grand piano that had been Great-Aunt Henrietta's pride and joy.

"Ver' well, if you wish it." She rose in a cloud of green mist and floated to the piano bench. Kellen glanced at the clock on the fireplace mantel—8:43. He hoped she would pick a long piece.

She forgot a Schubert waltz partway through, switched to Mozart, played too loud, then took up Beethoven's "Moonlight Sonata." Good. That would last some time.

At 9:06 p.m., she folded the lid down over the keyboard and returned to his side. "More chocolate?" she purred.

Kellen shook his head. He wanted no more chocolate. No more piano music. No more stilted conversation from this beautiful hothouse flower who had not one original thought in her head. He didn't think he could stand her oppressive closeness, the clinging, sweet scent of her ostentatiously displayed shoulders one more minute.

He wanted none of what she offered. Not from her. Something about her approach was too... accomplished. She professed innocence and feminine ineptitude, but Kellen knew better. She was an experienced huntress.

Nine-seventeen. Forty-three more minutes.

"Colonel," she murmured. "Ah feel a chill about mah shoulders. Do you mind if Ah cuddle up close?"

"I'll stir up the fire." He started to rise, but she clung to his arm.

"Ah'd rather you stayed heah," she whispered. "Next to me."

He grasped at a straw. "Would you care to read aloud? I just purchased a new volume of Longfellow."

"N-no, thank you. Ah prefer…conversation." She nestled her head against his shoulder. "Yoah so warm and strong."

He knew the next move, if he was so inclined. Lay his arm around her shoulders. Instead, he tented his hands on his thighs. Not, he noted with a flash of amusement, out of politeness. Out of disinterest.

Miss LeClair tilted her head, angling her mouth so if he leaned forward the slightest bit he would brush her lips. He sneaked another glance at the clock—9:23.

Oh, what the hell. He turned toward her, pressed his lips against hers. Her arm came around his neck and held him in a surprisingly strong grip. Then she opened her mouth under his, invited further invasion with her tongue, lapping at his like a hungry kitten.

He'd been here before with women. He knew it could lead to pleasure. For a moment he wondered at himself. Why not just accept what was offered and enjoy it?

He lifted his head and looked into Miss LeClair's eyes, hazy with desire, and suddenly he knew why. Because it wasn't enough. It would never be enough to simply share a woman's body and ignore the rest.

She pulled his head back to hers. "Again," she moaned. "Do it again."

Another meeting of mouth and tongue. The offer was so blatant he almost laughed. A military maneuver. A feminine feint, intended to outflank, capture and destroy.

Why not accept it?

Because it wouldn't last. Union of mouths and

tongues and bodies was one thing. Union of two spirits was another.

"Miss LeClair," he said after a decent interval. "Would you care to hear about the battle of Chancellorsville?"

He talked.

She listened.

He watched the hour hand creep toward deliverance. Finally he could take no more.

"I am afraid this evening must end." He lifted her hand from the back of his neck. "If this continues, you will be compromised."

"Oh, Ah do hope so," she whispered.

He rose, drew her up with him, gathered her shawl and walked her to the door. "I cannot allow your reputation to be sullied under my roof. Good night, Miss LeClair."

He signaled the waiting buggy driver, saw her safely ensconced and shut his front door with a satisfying thunk.

It was exactly 9:38 p.m.

Chapter Fourteen

The porch swing on the sun-drenched hotel veranda creaked back and forth four more times before Lolly could bring herself to ask the question that burned in her mind.

"Carrie, did Fleurette say anything when you stopped by the boardinghouse?"

"Not a word," Carrie replied. "Just rolled over and went back to sleep."

Concern warred with curiosity in Lolly's brain. "You don't think she's indisposed, do you?"

Carrie loosed a snort of laughter. "Most definitely not. Even half-asleep, she had the most satisfied smile on her face, as if she knew a big secret. Mrs. Petrov at the boardinghouse said she was just very, very tired."

Lolly stopped the motion of the swing. Fleurette did have a secret.

Carrie laid her small, capable hand on Lolly's forearm. "You fancy the colonel, don't you, Leora?"

Lolly waited until the blade of pain in her chest subsided. "I…like him, yes."

Carrie nodded and patted her arm sympathetically. "We ought to form an organization, like the Ladies Helpful Society. Call it Admirers of Colonel Macready. Or the Colonel's Ladies Brigade."

"Macready's Moths," Lolly offered.

Both of them burst into laughter, which faded as they spied Fleurette coming toward them.

The young woman lifted her voluminous pink gingham skirt and mounted the red-painted steps like a queen ascending her throne. "What y'all find so amusin'?"

Lolly and Carrie looked at each other a split second, then glanced away. "Men," Carrie answered.

"Women," Lolly said at the same instant.

Fleurette settled into a wicker armchair and propped her dainty leather slippers on a matching footstool. "Ah'm heah to tell y'all that Ah have found the man Ah'm goin' to wed."

"You must mean Colonel Macready," Lolly said dryly.

"We," Carrie said in a crisp tone, "have found him, too."

Fleurette went on as if she hadn't heard. "Wait till Ah tell 'bout last night with the colonel. My, he is *such* a fine gentleman!"

"A gentleman, yes," Carrie echoed. "Did he—?"

"Mah gracious, yes he did. A goodly number of times.

In fact, he became quite carried away and had to…" The calculating emerald eyes scanned their faces.

Lolly groaned inside. Fleurette had to make sure her audience was properly attentive. She had to admit she herself hung on every word Fleurette uttered, scarcely able to draw breath while the blade of pain sliced deeper into her heart. She couldn't stand the suspense much longer.

"Tell us."

"We..ll…" Fleurette drew the word out into two distinct syllables.

"Yes?" Carrie whispered. "And then he had to…what?"

Lolly didn't trust her own voice. If she opened her mouth she would scream in frustration. Blast the woman! Fleurette was actually enjoying this game. The cat lording it over the cream. Once again that primitive, predatory feeling blossomed in her belly.

Her hands twitched. She imagined her fingers around Fleurette's slim throat, squeezing the with-held words out past her lips. She massaged her knuckles.

Fleurette sighed. "Why, he had to stop himself for fear of ruinin' mah reputation." She lowered her voice to a murmur. "His passion was gettin' out of control, you see."

Carrie's eyes rounded. "Wh-what did he do? The passion part, I mean."

Lolly halted the rhythmically creaking swing to hear better.

"W…e…ll," Fleurette began. Three syllables this time. To keep her mind from exploding, Lolly shut her eyes and began to recite silently. *This is the forest primeval…*

"It was a very warm night, and…"

The murmuring pines and the…

"And after Ah played the piano for him—at his request, Ah might add—we…"

Lolly opened her eyelids and studied her hands. She could not play the piano. She could set type, but she had no musical training. No society skills. Surely a man of Colonel Macready's background and breeding would prefer a cultured, accom-plished woman for a wife? Someone who could entertain at the piano?

"He asked you to play for him?" Carrie said, her voice dreamy. "How wonderfully romantic! I can just picture it. He'd be standing behind you, his hands on your shoulders…. Is that how it was?"

The murmuring pines and the hemlocks…

Fleurette blinked. "Yoah not wantin' to scratch mah eyes out?"

"Of course not," Carrie said. "I just wish I'd thought of playing the piano. We played tiddledy-winks at the game table all evening."

A question zinged into Lolly's brain, and she twisted sideways to study Carrie's round, open face. *Carrie was not jealous? She* was jealous, Lolly admitted. Envious. Covetous. And a lot of other *"ous"*es.

Why *wasn't* Carrie jealous?

"As Ah was sayin', after the music, we…well, we sat close togetheh on the love seat, and then…" She let a beat of heavy silence go by.

Carrie leaned forward. "And then?"

"We began eatin' chocolate candy, and when he kissed me he tasted so sweet it made mah lips tingly." Fleurette gazed at the toes of her slippers and blushed prettily. "But he made 'em stop tingling after a while."

Tingling. The word itself burned into Lolly's

consciousness. ''Tingling'' was not what happened when Kellen had *kissed* her. Smacked in the chest by a sledgehammer was more like it.

''And then he lost control and was so carried away, Ah barely escaped in time.''

''Oh, my!'' Carrie breathed. She sucked in a tremulous gulp of air.

Oh, damn and blast, Lolly thought. She was out-maneuvered before she could even knock on the colonel's front door.

Well, so what? Even if Fleurette had captured his passions, Lolly could at least spend a pleasant evening in his company. Besides, recalling their last fiery encounter in his kitchen, she had a fence or two to mend.

Pain washed into her chest and then just as quickly ebbed away. She knew now there were worse things than being an old maid. She could be unable to read. She could be pregnant and unwed. She could be slandered. Ostracized from her home town, as she was sure Fleurette must have been.

Right then and there she made a decision. She would ask Orven Tillotsen for a position on his newspaper staff. She'd made her way on her own before; she could do it again.

All at once it didn't matter a bit what she wore

this evening. She was going to enjoy herself, and she need not dress up like a peacock to do it.

Goodness, she found her heart practically skipping. She could hardly wait!

"Well, now, Miss Leora. What can I do for you this morning?"

"Good day, Mr. Bodwin. I need an ice-cream freezer."

The mercantile owner's brows waggled. "I see. You own one-half of Matt Underwood's prize mare, I hear. Got baking rights in Mrs. Squires's kitchen, and now, 'cuz it's too hot to make cakes, it's ice cream and a freezer to make it. Sure a funny trousseau, if you take my meaning." He gave her a big grin. "Hard to keep up with you bride-ladies."

Lolly's heart jumped. "Oh?"

"Miss Careen, she bought out my entire stock of Demerara sugar for that cake, and that Miss LeClair comes in every day for a quart jar of kosher pickles and some lemon drops. Now it's an ice-cream freezer. You women are sure interesting. Whole town's watchin' every move you make."

Lolly gulped. "The whole town?"

"Yesirree. And certain gents most of all. What size freezer you fancy?"

"Which certain gents?"

"Well, Orv Tillotsen for one. I expect he's gathering tidbits for his newspaper. Sol Stanton and Gideon Hickmeyer—he owns the sawmill—hang around most every day hopin' for a glimpse of Miss LeClair. Sol's been buying so much pipe tobacco I'll have to reorder end of the week."

Now *that* was indeed interesting, Lolly thought.

"You want some rock salt with the freezer?"

Lolly jerked. "What? Oh, yes. Salt. And some…" She scanned the bushel baskets of fruit arranged at the front of the store, but her thoughts skittered off.

Sol Stanton, hoping for a glimpse of Fleurette?

Mr. Bodwin coughed politely. "And some what?"

"Yes, please. Four pounds should be sufficient."

Mr. Bodwin chuckled. "Four pounds of whatever I put in your basket, huh?"

But Lolly's attention was far away. Sol Stanton and Fleurette. The poor man. He was about to get his heart broken.

Her next stop was Mr. Tillotsen's small but tidy newspaper office on Main Street.

"A position on the *Gazette?*" The newspaperman's blue eyes nearly popped out of his head. "I thought you were one of the brides?"

"Colonel Macready cannot marry all three of us. I am simply being practical. Thinking ahead."

Mr. Tillotsen stroked the beginnings of a dark beard. "Mind if I ask your opinion on something, Miss Mayfield?"

Intrigued, Lolly gave him her full attention. "On what, Mr. Tillotsen?"

He swallowed audibly. "Orven," he said. "Anyone who can set type can call me by my Christian name."

"Very well, Orven. On what do you wish my opinion?"

He swallowed twice more. "Do you think Colonel Macready's going to marry Miss Careen?"

Lolly inspected the lean, tanned face across the desk. "Do you mean do I think Careen wishes to marry the colonel?" she said in a gentle voice.

"Matter of fact, Miss Mayfield, that is exactly what I mean."

"Leora, please. And forgive me if I speak too bluntly for such a delicate matter, but..."

Orven's face paled. "Of course, Miss...Leora. Just tell me before I bust."

"I think Careen has fancied herself in love with the colonel since she was a young girl."

The light went out of Orven's eyes, but he said nothing.

"But I do not believe she really cares for him." She spoke the words slowly, watching his face. "I believe Careen is enamored of the *idea* of being smitten with the colonel. Not with the colonel himself."

Orven bolted to his feet and grasped both her hands over the counter. "Do you honestly think so?"

"I honestly do." Lolly worked to keep the amusement from her voice. How unexpected life was! Orven Tillotsen was sweet on Careen Gundersen.

"And do you think I might gain a position on the *Gazette?*" she reminded.

His eyes refocused. "Oh, sure, Miss Leora. Anything you want."

"Five dollars a week."

"Granted."

"And a desk of my own."

"Naturally."

"And a regular column. Bylined." She held her breath.

"Do you write as well as you think?"

"Better." Lolly smiled and shook his hand. She had already composed the lead paragraph for her first column. Marriage in Maple Falls.

* * *

Leora turned in through the scrolled iron gate and proceeded up the walk to the front steps of the colonel's wide wraparound porch. Under her waist, her heart jumped and fluttered, and she had to work hard to control her breathing.

Pooh, what did it matter now? Everything was at sixes and sevens and upside down, as well. It was, she acknowledged with a ragged sigh, up to her to make her exit as graceful as she could; after all, if she intended to stay in Maple Falls, she must maintain good relations with both Carrie and Fleurette. No matter who ended up marrying the colonel.

Part of her felt philosophical about the situation. Maybe that was because she was used to facing things head-on, doing what must be done and moving on.

She'd learned that lesson early. She had just passed her fourteenth birthday when the news came about Papa. Killed at Chancellorsville when a young Rebel officer rallied his troops and surrounded the small, tired band of Federals caught behind enemy lines. They had been slaughtered to a man.

Lolly had grieved until she fell ill, and then, because her mother was ailing and someone had to keep the newspaper going, she tied on her father's printer's apron and stepped up to the job.

She did it for Papa. She resolved she would honor him and what he had stood for—a brave, lone voice for equality and freedom from slavery, for the truth as he saw it—with every ounce of strength and loyalty in her. She'd make Papa proud of her.

But deep down inside at this moment, another part of her felt the same gnawing loss about the colonel. She had known few men, outside of Papa, who measured up to Kellen Macready, even if he had been a Johnny Reb.

She stuffed down a sudden feeling of choking despair and raised one hand to the ornate metal door knocker. As the door swung open, Lolly said a quick prayer and straightened her shoulders.

"Good evening, Colonel Macready."

Kellen stared at Leora Mayfield, standing on his front porch with a basket of fresh peaches in one hand and some kind of wooden contraption in the other. She wore a simple skirt of blue percale and a frilly white blouse encrusted with lace at the neck.

"I'll need you to crank the ice-cream freezer, if you don't mind."

He lifted it, and the basket of peaches, from her

fingers, relieved that his hands were occupied. The urge to fold her into his arms was overwhelming. Good God, he was actually glad to see her! Extremely glad.

So glad that his heartbeat ratcheted into a warning drumroll.

Lolly unpinned her straw hat and laid it on a side table. "Is Mrs. Squires in?"

Kellen jerked. "Mrs. Squires? I thought you came to see *me?*"

"Yes, well I did, of course. I just thought since I'm going to use her kitchen—excuse me, *your* kitchen—I would speak to her first. It is only polite."

The prospect of having Leora bustling in his kitchen, or anywhere else in his house, pleased him more than he expected.

She looked up at him and smiled. "Will you be sufficiently entertained this evening if we make peach ice cream?"

She had very blue eyes, he noted again. More blue than the last time he had looked into their depths. Would they darken even more if he…?

Kellen, you fool. You idiot. You don't want to fall in love, remember? He didn't need his heart broken twice.

Leora brushed past him, through the dining room and into the kitchen. "Mrs. Squires?"

Kellen headed for the library and the brandy decanter. By the time he reached the kitchen, the place was redolent with the smell of ripe peaches.

Leora perched on a kitchen stool, a paring knife in her hand, while Mrs. Squires dunked one peach at a time into a kettle of boiling water and plopped it into an adjacent pan of cold water. Minnie Sullivan, their chaperone for the evening, fished out the fruit and handed it to Leora, who sliced it into a bowl with quick, sure motions. A pile of peach skins and pits mounded a plate before her.

"Would you care to help us?" Leora queried. "Dribble lemon juice over the slices?"

For some reason he felt irrationally happy to be included. He cut a lemon in half and squeezed some juice over the bowl.

"Shall we sing as we work?" Leora suggested.

Mrs. Squires beamed. "Oh, aye, lass. 'Comin' Through the Rye.' Her cracked voice rose. "'If a body meet a body...'"

Leora joined in, then Minnie. "'If a body kiss...'"

Kellen found himself singing, as well, pouring out the melody as if he had no care in the world but squeezing a lemon. "'All the laddies, have their lassies…'"

The growing mound of peach slices glistened. Then it was "Annie Laurie." And "Springfield Mountain." They ta-da'd the Irish Washerwoman jig until Minnie Sullivan began to dance, and when Leora and Mrs. Squires joined in, skirts hiked to their knees, Kellen thought maybe he'd had more brandy than he remembered. He had never heard such noise and laughter in this house.

Finally Leora dumped the cream and sugar and peach mixture into the freezer. Kellen packed the cavity with rock salt and carried the freezer out onto the back porch.

Leora followed, sat herself down beside him on the top step and watched him adjust the crank. The voices of Minnie Sullivan and Madge Squires drifted from the kitchen, singing "Long, Long Ago" and Kellen turned the handle in time with the music.

"I don't play the piano," Leora said suddenly.

"I do. But I don't know how to set type."

"I do." She waited until she couldn't stand it one more second. "Mr. Tillotsen told you, didn't he?"

"He did. He didn't intend to, I think. He was talking about—" He stopped. Orven had spoken to him in confidence.

"About Careen Gundersen," Leora said quietly. "I think…"

"So do I," Kellen said. "I couldn't have chosen her anyway. She's a lovely girl, but…" The sound of a tiddledywink chunking into a glass echoed in his brain so clearly, he laughed out loud.

"When your arm gets tired, I will crank."

Kellen's arm ached, but not from turning the freezer handle. He wanted to wrap it around Leora, pull her close and smell her hair. His hand slowed.

Without a word, she took over the crank and began to hum "Pop Goes the Weasel" along with the women inside. She churned so hard he had to steady the freezer base between his hands, watching her arm and shoulder move under the soft white muslin.

"Why did you really go to the newspaper office, Leora?"

Her rhythm broke for just an instant. "Didn't Orven tell you?"

"He talked mostly about Careen. About what you'd told him."

Kellen waited. He didn't want to push or pry. But he had to know.

"I asked him about employment." She cranked harder. "In case I don't get—"

"Get occupied otherwise," he finished.

"Married," she corrected. "To you. There is no point in mincing words."

"Would that be your preference?"

"Which? Writing a newspaper column or marrying you?"

Her turning hand stopped. "I cannot answer that question yet."

"Aha." It was all he could think of to say.

"You're the reason I'm in this fix in the first place. When Papa was killed, I took over the newspaper in Baxter Springs, and then Mama got sick and…"

"Aha," he said again.

"I had to do something just to survive, but I missed out on…everything. That's why I came to Maple Falls."

"I see."

"I don't think you do. Not entirely."

"Miss Mayfield?"

"Yes, Colonel Macready?"

He lifted her hand from the freezer handle. "May I kiss you?"

"I think you'd better not. We always get into a fight afterward." She went back to cranking.

"Leora?" Again he lifted her hand away.

"Yes, Kellen?"

He bent toward her. "It's worth it."

Chapter Fifteen

The instant his lips touched hers, Kellen knew it was a mistake to kiss her. Even when she moaned in his embrace and propriety demanded that he release her, he did not want to stop.

He would never want to stop. The realization turned his blood into hot molasses. Still, he continued to explore her mouth until his veins heated to molten silver.

"Kellen, stop. Remember the ice cream."

"To hell with the ice cream," he whispered against her cheek. He caught a whiff of her scent, light and fresh, like the sweet peas Mrs. Squires planted along the back fence.

Leora gave the wooden freezer a halfhearted pat, then brought her hand to his chest. "I understand you iron your shirts yourself."

The statement seemed provocatively irrelevant, considering the circumstances. "I do, yes."

"This one is going to get all wrinkled again."

Kellen laughed softly. "I sure as hell hope so." He kissed her again. She twisted toward him, ran her warm fingers into his hair and his heart stuttered to a stop. The sensation was so arousing it stopped his breath, as well. Gently he loosened the clasp securing the bun of dark hair at her neck.

"My hair," she said. "It's coming unpinned."

"What a good idea," he murmured in a voice not quite his own. Some other man was speaking through him, some other man who could take what she offered and fear no consequences from giving his heart to a woman.

"Leora."

She said nothing, just pulled his head down and held it against her breast. Beneath his ear her heart raced. His mind cried her name while his body hungered.

"Kellen, we must not… What will Mrs. Squires think? And Minnie Sullivan?"

"Madge Squires will dance a jig," he said against her mouth. "She's the only one whose opinion I care about. Other than you." He nipped her ear, her chin, pressed his lips against her closed eyelids.

"Would you care to—stop, Kellen—know what my opinion is at this moment?"

He lifted his head. "Something tells me you're going to tell me anyway, sooner or later."

"Yes, I am."

"If it's something I don't want to hear, I'd rather it be later."

"Turn the freezer handle," she whispered. "Otherwise we'll have slush."

He rotated her shoulders, settled her spine back against his chest and reached around her for the crank. "Ice cream," he said against her temple, "is the only thing keeping me sane at the moment."

She turned her head sideways, brushed her lips against his cheek. "You feel quite sane, then? Doing this? I don't."

"I want to unbutton your blouse," he said.

"You cannot," she said softly. "You're making peach ice cream."

He drew back to look at her. "Did you know this would happen?"

"Only the ice cream part. The other, no."

He brushed his palm down the soft white sleeve of her blouse. "What are you wearing underneath this?"

Her voice, when she replied, was soft, with a

hint of laughter. "That is a most improper question."

"Yes," he said. "I've never said these things to a woman."

"You are a brave man, Kellen."

"Far from it. I am more terrified at this moment than I ever was during the war."

"I guessed that," she said. "I know that this—us—frightens you."

"It does, yes. What you don't know is how much."

"I think I do."

"Leora." He angled her chin toward his mouth. "Don't talk. Kiss me."

"Kellen...Kellen? You like me, do you not." It wasn't a question, more an observation. Her voice was uneven.

"You know I do."

"You don't want to, but you do."

"Yes. I like you. And more. The minute I kissed you in the gazebo that night I knew I was in trouble. Dammit, Leora, I'm falling in love with you."

"Against your will," she said softly.

"Yes." He stopped turning the freezer handle and tightened both arms around her. "But it's there, just the same."

"For me, as well," she breathed.

"Damn. The ice cream is ready."

Leora laughed. "Oh, Kellen, do you know what I want right now?"

He just looked at her. In a thousand years he couldn't imagine what this woman would want at this moment. What she would say next. What she was thinking.

"I want three—no, four—things." Her voice was so soft he could scarcely hear her.

"Name the first. I'll see what I can do."

She opened her mouth to speak, hesitated, opened it again. "I want to take off all my clothes while you watch."

His groin began to ache.

"I want you to touch me."

"That's two," he said, his voice rough.

"I—I want you to choose Fleurette LeClair."

Kellen set her away from him. "Are you crazy? I don't care a feather about Fleurette."

"Exactly," Leora said. "You will be safe. You won't ever suffer."

"What makes you think that's what I want?"

"You are right to be frightened, in a way. When two people care about each other, they can hurt each other. I don't ever want to hurt you. I think I love you, Kellen. And that makes us both vulnerable."

He shook his head in bewilderment. "That is complete and total nonsense." He spread her hand, turned it over and kissed her palm.

"Quite possibly," Lolly said when she could draw breath. "But it is human nature all the same."

"You want me to choose Fleurette. Choose safety over risk, is that it?"

"Fleurette's need is greater than mine."

"What about *my* need?"

"Oh, Kellen. I believe that *is* what you need. What you want underneath."

"What's the fourth thing you want?"

She sent him a smile that flooded his entire body with heat.

"A big, big bowl of peach ice cream. And two spoons."

"There is something else I want as well," Lolly announced as she laid her spoon beside Kellen's in the empty Wedgwood bowl.

"Name it. I will try not to be surprised."

"I want you to take me fishing."

"Fishing!" His face looked so thunderstruck Lolly almost laughed aloud.

"In one of the boats down by your dock. We discovered them during the Bramble Scramble."

"Fishing," he reiterated. "As in hooks? Worms? Poles? *Worms?*"

He repeated "worms" twice, Lolly noted.

"Yes, Kellen, with worms. Oh, don't look so shocked— I've been fishing many times. My father and I would go down to a little lake not far from Baxter Springs. On really hot days, I sometimes went swimming."

"Swimming," Kellen repeated. He had the oddest look, as if someone had smacked him over the head with an umbrella.

"After we'd caught our fish, of course. Otherwise the splashing frightened away the fish."

Kellen studied her face. "There are plenty of things I'd like to do at this moment, but fishing isn't one of them. Fishing hasn't even made the list."

"Please, Kellen. Just this once. Before…" She closed her lips over the rest of the sentence. Before he was married, she was going to say. But, oh, Lord, she couldn't bring herself to utter those particular words.

"Kellen?"

"When? Tomorrow I have to—"

"Now. Tonight."

"Tonight? Leora, you can't be serious."

"Of course I am serious. The moon is so full I

can see all the way to your lath house, over there.'' She pointed her index finger in the direction of the purple clematis-covered structure.

Kellen stretched his legs full-length down the porch steps. ''Yes, I can see it, as well. That's where my great-aunt Henrietta used to start her rhubarb seedlings in midwinter.'' He hoped the mention of Aunt Henrietta, or seedlings or *something* would distract her attention away from fishing.

Leora's eyes lit up with interest. ''She grew rhubarb?''

''She did, yes. When I first came out to Oregon after the war, I thought it was tobacco.''

Lolly smiled up at him. ''Would your aunt have planted tobacco?''

''Not unless she was blind.'' The thought of his great-aunt in her lace-encrusted black dress out in the garden cutting and drying tobacco made him chuckle. ''That's why she left Virginia in the first place. Her husband grew tobacco and kept slaves to work the fields. Aunt Henrietta had always been against slavery, even before the war.''

Leora cocked her head. ''Tell me more about your aunt Henrietta.''

Kellen bit back a smile. His ploy was working; Leora had lost interest in the fishing expedition.

"Aunt Henrietta was an upstanding pillar of the Methodist church, a fine pianist and a wicked poker player."

"Poker! She played cards? I thought the Methodists..."

"They do disapprove. But Aunt Henrietta took pity on me when I came out to live with her after the war. She let me teach her five-card stud. She thought she was doing a wounded Reb soldier a favor."

Leora touched his arm. "You were wounded?"

Kellen swallowed and looked away. He'd said too much. Even now he didn't like to talk about the scars he carried inside, on his soul. "Nothing to worry the nurses too much," he said lightly.

She leaned away from him, studying his face. The look in her eyes made him nervous.

"Did you know you can't grow good lettuce in Kansas? It's so hot in the summer it bolts and goes to seed before you can pick it."

He shook his head. The subject had changed so quickly he wasn't sure he'd heard her right. "Lettuce? Did you say 'lettuce'?"

She nodded and sent him a smile that kicked up his heartbeat. "I did. And now," she continued in a businesslike tone, "let's get back to fishing, shall we?"

He could hear the laughter in her voice. Worse, he could see the determination in her blue eyes. A man was helpless before her.

Kellen rose, lifted the ice cream freezer and the two empty bowls and carried them through the screen door into the kitchen. Mrs. Squires beamed at him and plopped the dishes into the sink.

He escaped to the back porch to find Leora coiling her hair into its loose bun. "Damn," he murmured. He didn't want to drop fishing lines in the river; he wanted to tangle his fingers in that mass of dark hair. He wanted—

"The blue boat," Leora announced. "It's more of a moonlight color than red or yellow."

A more single-minded woman he had never encountered. "Very well, the blue boat. Shall I dig a few worms, or would you prefer to do it?" Instantly he regretted his challenge. A man, even an exasperated, annoyed, aching man, should not take out his pique in spoken barbs. He opened his lips to apologize, but she cut him off.

"I will dig the worms," she announced. "I like worms."

Kellen stared at her so long her grin slowly disappeared. "Years from now," he said in a low voice, "I will look back on this evening and I won't believe any of it."

Her smile returned. ''Years from now, I trust we will be friends. And I will remind you that it most certainly did happen.

''And the best part,'' she continued in a light, lilting tone, ''is that it's not over yet.''

Chapter Sixteen

The blue rowboat glistened as if unseen hands had polished it with moonlight. Skimming down the wooden dock, Lolly stopped suddenly and tried to etch the scene in her memory. She was glad she had asked for the blue boat; blue was her favorite color. She would remember this night all the rest of her life.

"Look," she breathed as Kellen caught up to her. "It looks the way I always imagined Lohengrin's boat would be."

"I thought Lohengrin rode a swan to the Grail castle," Kellen said with a laugh.

"A swan-boat," she said softly. "This will be our swan-boat."

He stood at her back, close enough that his warm breath fanned the back of her neck when he chuckled. "Kind of fancy for you and me and a couple of trout, don't you think?"

She ached to take one step backward and press her body against his, her shoulder blades against his chest, her bottom against his thighs. Great stars in heaven, she'd never had such a thought in her entire life! And that feeling inside her...well, she'd never had that before, either.

"There's something magical about this night," she murmured.

He spoke near her ear. "It's the worms," he whispered.

Lolly jerked. She held the tin of wriggling bait in both hands.

"Maybe we ate too many," Kellen added.

She hiccuped a laugh and turned toward him. "You want some more?" She extended the tin can toward him.

She expected him to laugh, but he groaned instead. Then he lifted the bait out of her hands, set the can on the wooden dock and straightened.

"Miss Mayfield?" His voice was lower than usual, almost hoarse.

"Colonel Macready?"

"You are the damnedest woman." He pulled her tight against him. "But don't change, Leora. Don't ever change."

For a moment Lolly could think of nothing but the feel of his body pressed to hers, the power in the arms that enfolded her, the heat of his thighs.

Every inch of him was resisting her as a woman. She knew that. Reveled in it. She knew it wasn't kind to tease; she had suggested fishing to give them something to occupy their hands and minds other than what she now knew they both wanted.

He bent his head, touched his mouth to hers. His firm, warm lips tasted of peaches and, oh God, she wanted more. His tongue tracing the outline of her mouth felt smooth and hot and deliberate, and then he stroked in, and out.

She closed her eyes. Her breasts swelled. Ached. *Again,* she pleaded silently. *Do it again.*

He broke away with a groan and held her apart from him.

"Trout," he murmured, his voice uneven.

Lolly sighed and opened her lids to see raw hunger in his eyes. "Lohengrin," she whispered. "The boat."

He stepped away, snugged the boat to the end of the dock and set the bait can and two fishing poles in the bottom. Then he righted the oars, put one foot on the dock and one in the vessel and reached for her hand.

His fingers shook as he helped her step down

into the boat. She made her way carefully to the end bench and sat down facing him. The soft night air smelled of jasmine, so sweet and elusive she lifted her face and opened her mouth to capture it.

Kellen stepped into the boat. Just as he was about to push off, Sam padded down the dock and jumped in with them.

With Sam sprawled at his feet, he took up the oars. But he didn't look at Sam, or the oars, or even at the river. He looked straight at Lolly.

They drifted in silence for a time, letting the gentle current float them down river a few yards before Kellen gradually rowed the craft back to its starting point.

"River widens up ahead," he said. "Not much current." He stroked for a few minutes, then let the boat drift in lazy circles. The water rippled silver where the oars cut it.

Without a word, Lolly baited a hook and dropped her line into the smooth water. Kellen watched her, a bemused smile playing on his lips. Maybe he'd never been fishing at midnight with a dog who worshiped him and a woman who...

Lolly sucked in a breath. Never mind that now. She sat not four feet away from him, but she could feel his heat, his maleness. To keep her thoughts under control she drew in her line, checked the hook and slung it out over the water again.

Still Kellen watched her.

"Aren't you going to bait your hook?"

His chuckle rumbled into the velvety dark. "What makes you think I haven't?"

She knew instantly what he meant. How could she be even this close to him, floating on their private lake, dappled with moonlight, and not feel the pull she knew he referred to?

It was an age-old yearning, as inescapable as nature itself. She had read enough books in the Baxter Springs library to recognize a mating ritual when she saw it. Experiencing it was even more thrilling, like the call of a long unheard voice deep inside her.

Lolly was glad they were in the boat, separated by Sam and a few dozen lightning bugs. But oh, how she ached for him.

Kellen guided the craft noiselessly in a wide, slow circle, his oar dipping into the water in silence. Good to have his hands occupied. He'd work to keep them that way.

He oared to the left, watched the dark water ripple in their wake. When the boat angled into the breeze, he could catch drifts of her scent. Vanilla, and something richer, more earthy beneath that.

The fragrance caught at his senses, penetrated so deep he could taste it in his throat. His groin.

Heaven help him. It was all right as long as they were sitting quietly in the boat, Lolly at one end, himself at the other. What about afterward?

"Oh! I've got one!" Lolly's voice rose with excitement. She reeled in the line and gasped. "Look how big it is!"

The fish—a brown trout, Kellen guessed—flopped into the boat and in the next moment two unexpected things happened.

Leora stood up to unhook her catch, and Sam bolted toward her. She teetered, stumbled to the left and Sam followed.

Kellen could see what was going to happen. With both Sam and Leora on the far left, the little craft was unbalanced.

They were going over.

"Sam!" Kellen shouted at the rambunctious dog nuzzling Leora's skirt. "Come here."

Too late. The small craft tipped on its side, dumping both Leora and Sam into the river. Kellen leaned to the left, reached an oar toward the spot he'd last seen them as the boat rolled on over with a resounding splash. Kellen found himself in the river, as well.

"Leora! Sam!" His throat went dry. Why had they not surfaced?

The boat floated, bottom side up, just beyond his reach. Without conscious thought he dove beneath the surface, groping in the murky water for a piece of clothing, an arm, anything. When his lungs screamed for air he resurfaced to gulp in a life-saving breath.

He pulled another deep breath into his lungs and arched to dive again when a head popped up, followed by a dog. The relief that swept over him was so sweet he felt a sob rise from his belly.

Sam dog-paddled toward him, and Leora... Good God, she was not drowning, she was laughing!

He swam toward her, resisting the impulse to grab her shoulders and shake her until her senses returned.

"Don't look so worried," she sputtered. "I told you I often swim when I go fishing. Doesn't the water feel delicious?"

Kellen watched her expertly tread water and gritted his teeth. "Get to the boat," he ordered. Sam, swimming steadily, was already halfway to the bank.

"The boat," he shouted. He managed a strong

kick and sidestroked beside her until they reached the overturned craft.

She was still laughing. Kellen pulled himself up onto the rounded hull and swung his weight forward. The boat tipped, hovered precariously for a moment, and then plopped right side up onto the river surface. He guessed air had been trapped underneath; otherwise it would have swamped.

He hauled the top part of his torso over the edge, grabbed the oar lock and pulled the rest of his sodden body into the vessel. Kneeling in the hull, he braced his legs under the bench seat and reached his trembling arms out to Leora.

"I'm too heavy to pull in, Kellen. My skirt weighs me down."

He grasped her wrist. "Take your skirt off. And your petticoat. And don't argue."

"I'm too tired to argue. But it *is* funny, don't you think?"

For the life of him he couldn't see the humor in it. All he could think about was the awful, empty feeling in the pit of his stomach when he'd watched her head disappear under the surface.

"Kellen, you have to let go of my wrist. I can't undo the buttons with only one hand."

It took all his willpower to release his hold on her. While she fumbled and splashed in the river, he prayed the way he had when he was a boy. *Save her, God. Let her live.*

A squishy ball of blue cotton flopped near his knees, followed by a smaller lump of ruffly white.

"I'm ready," she sang.

"Lie alongside the boat. Just float there."

She obeyed without hesitation, stretching out on her back and letting the river support her. With the water glistening on her skin, her hands gently sculling at her sides, she looked like an exotic white fish.

He reached both hands under her waist. "Grab my neck."

He took a breath, then heaved upward with all his strength and muscled her body up over the side. He winced when he heard her clothing rasp against the wood. It would be worse on her bare skin, but he couldn't afford to think about it now.

At last one shoulder cleared the edge, then her knees, and finally she toppled in on top of him.

For a moment they just lay entwined in the bottom of the boat, panting to catch their breath. Finally Leora opened her eyes and looked up at him.

"Where is my fish?"

"Swimming back to his sweetheart," Kellen answered.

"Oh." Her disappointment was so obvious he

tried hard to keep his lips from twitching into a grin.

He also tried hard not to notice how their chilled bodies were still plastered together, and how warm and pleasant he was beginning to feel at the contact. Her breasts pressed onto his chest, and he felt her nipples harden through the wet muslin of her camisole.

Water still dripped off his shirt, and two buttons were missing. He heard her breathing change, but he did not move.

"I've lost my shoes!"

She sounded so delighted, Kellen had to laugh. "I lost mine, as well."

"They were my fancy jab-toed shoes," she said happily. "I hated them!"

Kellen lowered his head and spoke into her ear. "Do you realize we're having this conversation soaking wet in the bottom of a rowboat?"

"Why, of course." She pronounced the words slowly, deliberately, and he heard quiet amusement in her voice.

"I think it's been a wonderful evening, Kellen. I hope you have been sufficiently entertained."

He laughed, then kissed her, and kissed her again, deeper. "We should get out of these wet clothes," he murmured.

"Yes, I suppose so," Lolly said on a sigh. "Take our clothes off." The word echoed in her brain.

"We need to get dry."

She rolled off his chest and sat up. When the breeze touched her wet skin, she began to shiver. "Here? In the boat?"

He was silent so long she wondered if he'd changed his mind.

"No," he said at last. "Up at the house, where it's warm. The stove in the kitchen will still be hot."

"Goodness, what will Mrs. Squires think?"

Kellen chuckled. "She'll think we fell into the river and got dunked. Madge Squires is like an owl—she sees things very clearly. Especially at night."

Lolly began wringing water out of her blue skirt and petticoat. "What about Minnie Sullivan?"

He glanced up at the night sky. "It's well past midnight. Mrs. Sullivan is no doubt snuggled in bed with Mr. Sullivan."

Lolly smiled. "Very well, then. Your kitchen." She gathered up her sodden garments, stepped to the bench seat in the rear of the boat and sat down facing him.

Without speaking, he settled himself behind the

oars and rowed downstream toward the dock. Lolly watched the muscles in his arms and shoulders flex under the clingy wet shirt. She tried to think about his warm, welcoming kitchen, about how she would manage to dry her clothes in the same room with Kellen. And vice versa. A blush heated her skin from her neck to her hairline. Thank the Lord he couldn't see her face in the dark.

Inexplicably he began to sing softly. "I gave my love a fish..."

Lolly burst out with a shuddery laugh. The air was beginning to feel really cold now. Funny, it didn't seem to bother Kellen. His low voice continued the impromptu song without a quaver. "She tossed it in the river..."

Lolly guessed he was trying to keep her spirits up. While she loved the sound of Kellen's rich baritone, she didn't really need her spirits raised. Her spirits were as up as they could get, even if she was freezing in the back end of a rowboat.

It *had* been a wonderful evening. A glorious, funny, unforgettable evening. She wanted it to go on and on so she could savor every precious moment through the long years ahead. The long *unmarried* years ahead.

"She fell into the water..." Laughter colored his voice, sending a warmth into her soul.

She loved this man. And she suspected he loved her, even though he didn't want to. Even though he was afraid of loving her, of getting hurt as he had years ago. Her throat tightened. This would be the last night on this earth she would ever spend with him.

The boat bumped up against the dock. Kellen leaped out, secured the rope, then stepped back in and extended his hand. Very carefully he walked her to the front of the craft, keeping her hand in his until they both stood shivering on the dock.

A bedraggled Sam padded toward them and nuzzled Kellen's free hand. The other Kellen kept entwined with Lolly's.

"I'm sorry it's over," she said.

"I'm not." The laughter was gone from his voice. "I don't know how much more I could have stood."

Lolly knew exactly what he meant.

Hands still clasped, they walked the long wooden dock to the lawn that grew down to the riverfront. Their bare feet squished across the grass until they reached the back porch, where a lantern had been left to light their way.

The first thing Kellen did was to puff out the flame. Then he moved to the kitchen stove and stirred up the banked coals. In the firelight's glow

Lolly watched him remove his shirt and drape it over the back of a wooden chair. Then he came toward her, singing under his breath. "She dried off in the kitchen..."

He caught her to him and held her without speaking for a long minute. "I'll bring you a robe," he said at last. He brushed her cheek with his lips and was gone.

In ten minutes he was back, fully dressed in a dry shirt and trousers. "Here's a towel for your hair."

Her hair! Great heavens, she hadn't given it a single thought. She must look worse than Sam!

Kellen handed her a soft flannel robe, gave her a long look and turned his back. Quickly she removed her white muslin waist, camisole and underdrawers and donned the robe. That done, she stepped to the sink and squeezed out the garments.

His robe smelled like him—a dark, spicy scent of pipe smoke mixed with pine soap. She laid the garments across the warming stove plates. She hung her underdrawers in the warming oven.

She wanted, desperately wanted, for Kellen to touch her. Kiss her. But she knew instinctively that he would not. Not here. Not like this, with her naked but for his robe. Honorable men were...well, honorable.

She admired that quality in him. But at this moment it was driving her senses into a frenzy.

This is our last time together.

She paced the kitchen, the wash porch, the backyard, breathing in the sharp, clean scent of grass mixed with the underlying sweetness of honeysuckle. Time seemed to pass so slowly she envisioned greeting Mrs. Squires when she arrived in the morning to cook breakfast.

On her final circuit of the yard, the back screen door flapped open and Kellen's hand emerged, proffering a bouquet of dry clothes.

Everything but her petticoat ruffle was dry as toast. While Kellen waited on the back porch steps, she dressed slowly, reluctant to return to the real world.

When she had combed her fingers through her still-damp hair, she wound it back into a soft bun, secured it with some metal poultry stuffing skewers she found in a drawer and walked outside to Kellen.

He sat on the steps with his back to her, his long legs stretched out before him. His dark head was bent, his forehead resting in one palm. Lolly knew his eyes would be closed.

A violent wave of sweet-hot pain surged through her chest, down to her thighs. At that moment, she knew what she wanted, and she wanted it more than anything on earth.

She sat down beside him. "Kellen."

"I know," he said. "Just a few more minutes."

"Kellen, I want you to walk me home, through the field of lavender behind the Underwood place."

He looked up. "In the middle of the night? Are you sure?"

"It's a heavenly warm night."

"Leora…?"

"I want us to walk slowly. Very, very slowly. Will you?"

He held her gaze for a long minute. "I'll just check the stove, and get my jacket."

By the time they reached the path through the lavender field, Lolly was so full of longing she scarcely knew what she was doing. Or what she was saying. Every few yards their footsteps slowed and then stopped, and Kellen pulled her close. Drunk with joy, she said whatever came into her mind. Did whatever she felt impelled to do.

He kissed her, undid the buttons of her blouse and touched her skin, his breathing ragged and his mouth hungry. His fingers trembled when he cupped her face, then his tongue was hot and sure against her nipples, making her ache for him.

Halfway through the field he stopped, took off

his jacket and laid it out on the lush purple blooms. Then he removed his shirt and spread it flat.

"I can't take you, you know that," he said in a quiet voice. "But I want to see you. I want to touch you."

Lolly held his hands against her breasts, feeling heat sizzle through muslin and lace until her knees weakened. "I want something from you, as well," she whispered. "Something only you can give me."

"Not a child. You don't think I—"

"No, not a child. But something for myself. Something I can remember for the rest of my life."

"Anything," he whispered. "Anything within my power."

"I want you to undress me. All the way."

His breath shuddered in, and she smiled up at him. "And there's more."

"What 'more'? I'm halfway afraid of your 'mores.'"

"I want to feel you."

He stared at her, his eyes darkening. "How do you mean?"

"Inside me. I want you to be the first."

"Good heavens, Leora, do you know what you're saying?"

"I do. Do you know what I am asking?"

"Yes." His voice shook.

"Do you want it, Kellen? I know it is a risk. Not because of a child, but because you are afraid of losing something, someone, you care for."

"Stop, Leora. Don't say any more." He held her, pressed her head into his shoulder. She could feel his body tremble with desire, as hers did.

"Do you know how terrifying it is to stand before the woman you—" He broke off.

"You are so afraid of loss you will not risk marrying for love. I understand that, Kellen. I accept it."

"How can you do this? Want this?" he said in a voice that broke.

She stopped his words with her lips. "Because my price for giving you up is very high."

She stood quietly while he slipped the rest of the buttons free and slid the muslin blouse off her shoulders. He untied the ribbon of her white cotton camisole, kissing her breasts and nipples as he pushed it down.

"There has never been anyone like you, Leora. Never."

"You have had other women," she said in a low voice. "Show me what to do."

"Nothing. Do nothing. Let me." He freed the waistband of her skirt and let it drop to her ankles, followed by her soft, lacy petticoat. He shed his trousers and underdrawers, then knelt before her.

"For me," she said softly, "there will never be anyone but you."

He turned her, kissed the backs of her knees, the inside of her thighs. "I don't want that for you. I want you to marry. To be happy."

"I am happy. I am happier tonight than I have ever been."

Kellen buried his face against her belly. "I feel like I'm being cut in two. I've never been closer to another human being, and I've never been more frightened."

Lolly's heart lurched. She mattered to him! That was all she needed to know, all she wanted. He could marry anyone he cared to; she knew she would always hold a piece of his heart.

She sank onto his spread-out jacket, pulling him with her until they lay entwined together.

"Show me, Kellen," she whispered. "Now."

Chapter Seventeen

He made it slow and sweet. Lolly never dreamed such exquisite feelings were possible just from a man's touch. His hands smoothed her skin, caressed her hips, her breasts, until her entire body burned. When he touched her most intimate place, gently drawing his finger back and forth over her aching flesh, she felt as if she were soaring outside of herself.

His breath rasped in and his mouth sought her nipples, then her lips. His hot, slick tongue moved past her teeth, urging her to open to him, urging not only with his lips and tongue, but with his fingers on her soft inner folds, mimicking the stroking of his tongue inside her mouth. She began to move under him.

She gasped, arching under his hands and heard

her own voice cry out. Sounds she never dreamed she could utter escaped her lips. Oh, what sweet relief to let the hunger and the yearning out of the prison of propriety. It was almost holy, sharing this much of one's inner self and one's physical being with another human. With a man.

Kellen's breathing grew throaty and uneven as she moaned in pleasure, and suddenly she wanted to feel him inside her, wanted to give him the same thrill of possession she felt. It was conquest, pure and simple. Elemental and powerful. Animal in its driving intent, spiritual in the resulting ultimate connection.

He rose over her, then straddled her. She heard him breathe her name, and then he pushed hard into her, past the dart of pain that brought a gasp to her lips. Then he began to move inside her, slowly, deliberately exploring the waiting depths within her. Under her fingers she felt the muscles bunch in his naked back. Sweat slicked his heated skin, and hers, as well, she thought fleetingly. It didn't matter. Nothing mattered.

She urged him deeper, heard him begin to lose control.

"Leora," he panted. "Don't…move."

But she could not stop. Did not want to stop. If

this was all she would ever have of him, she wanted everything he had to give.

She raised her head, met his open mouth with hers. Something built inside her, a sweet tension that impelled her onward, to belong wholly to him.

He lost himself in thrusting, and then stiffened and cried out.

Weeping now, she held him close and tight inside her until spasm after spasm of exquisite, breath-stopping pleasure rippled deep in her center.

"Kellen!"

"Oh, Leora, I meant to withdraw."

"Don't leave me." She contracted her inner muscles around his hard length, heard him suck in air.

He thrust again, a lazy plunge into her depths, and she convulsed once more.

"Again," she whispered.

"Leora. Leora, I love you."

"Again."

She smiled up at him. "Again."

Near dawn they awoke, their skin smelling of lavender and the musky scent of lovemaking. Without a word they dressed and held each other until the sky turned from slate to peach. Then Lolly straightened her skirt and smoothed her hair into a bun, which Kellen helped her pin up.

As the rim of the sun appeared over the mountains in the distance, they clung to each other without speaking. Then Lolly wrenched herself free and started down the path toward the hotel. Kellen slung his rumpled jacket over one shoulder and stood watching her until the rose-gold light blurred his vision.

"Mah gracious sakes, Leora, it's not like you to be late for lunch." The voice came from behind an upright copy of the *Golden Valley Gazette,* propped between two small white hands.

"Why, just listen to this!" Careen said from behind an identical newspaper. "Oh, good afternoon, Leora. It says here that Dora Mae Landsfelter and Colonel Macready will make an announcement from the hotel veranda this evening."

"Oh?" Lolly set her curiously light body down on the empty dining chair.

"You don't sound the slightest bit interested," Carrie said.

She was interested, all right. She already knew the outcome—Kellen would choose Fleurette to be his bride. The question weighing on Lolly's mind at this moment was whether she could walk into

Mr. Tillotsen's newspaper office the following morning and start to work as if nothing had happened. Not two weeks ago all she'd wanted was to get married and save herself from being an old maid for the rest of her life.

But that was before Kellen.

Now all she wanted was for Kellen to be happy. However he wanted.

"My," Carrie said with a sigh. "Orven Tillotsen does have a lovely way with words. Just listen to this. 'The sun in all its radiance cannot match the beauty of Miss Careen Gundersen and the other two young women awaiting final results of the Ladies Helpful Society's bride competition.'"

"Very poetical," Fleurette said in a dry voice.

"And selective," Lolly added, keeping her attention on Carrie's animated face.

"You sure he didn't mention mah name?"

"You can read it for yourself," Carrie answered. "It's right there below the letters to the editor."

Lolly forgot her gnawing hunger as she watched Fleurette's clever fakery with the newspaper in her hands. "Yes, Ah see now. Very poetical indeed." She lowered the newsprint to meet Lolly's gaze across the luncheon table.

"Mah stars, Leora, you look pos'tively..."

Carrie glanced up. "Different," she pronounced.

"Kind of lit up from the inside. You haven't been nipping at Mr. Bodwin's applejack, have you?" Her brow furrowed in motherly concern.

"I...did not sleep much last night," Lolly confessed.

Fleurette leaned toward her. "Here, have some of mah coffee, Leora, then tell us all about it."

"Oh, yes, do," Carrie sang. She signaled the waitress, "How many times did he—" She broke off as the gingham-aproned girl approached with her pad and pencil.

"I will have the creamed chicken," Carrie announced. She glanced sideways at the newspaper while Fleurette gave her order.

"Ah want what Ah had yesterday. A chicken croquette, wasn't it? Just one."

"Ham and eggs and potatoes and a double order of toast," Lolly blurted without thinking.

Fleurette and Carrie stared at her. "You haven't had yoah breakfast yet?"

"I slept late," Lolly said quickly.

"Because of last night with the colonel?" Carrie's voice was hushed in awe.

Fleurette's eyes flashed. "Whateveh did y'all do?"

Lolly gulped. "We made ice cream and sang

songs. And…talked some.'' It was perfectly true, as far as it went.

Fleurette settled back in her dining chair with a satisfied sigh. ''Well, that caint have been too tirin'.''

''No, it wasn't, not at all. It was—'' *You goose! You can't say a single word about what really happened.* Not, and live in Maple Falls with these women as friends and neighbors for years to come.

''—enlightening,'' she finished.

Carrie sent her a look of heartfelt sympathy. ''Sounds pretty awful. Like conjugating verbs.''

''Poor Leora,'' Fleurette murmured. ''Don't know the first thing 'bout bein' with a man, do you, honey?''

''Not the first thing,'' Lolly agreed. She willed herself to keep a straight face. She did, however, know the second, third and fourth things.

And the fifth, sixth and on up to a hundred, as well. She had learned it all in just one night. Even more startling was what she had discovered about herself.

''It says here the colonel's engagement will be announced this evening!'' Carrie read aloud.

Lolly's butter knife clanked onto her plate and the slice of toast cartwheeled end over end onto the tablecloth.

Fleurette sniffed.

Lolly snatched up the toast and crunched her teeth into it. "It landed butter side up," she quipped, praying neither woman would not notice her shaking fingers.

Why was she so nervous? She knew what the outcome would be; she had known for days, ever since Carrie had given them each half of the mare the schoolteacher had won in the Bramble Scramble.

Lolly and Fleurette would share something else, as well. Lolly had claimed her share last night. For the rest of her days, she would live on those memories while Fleurette lived as Kellen's wife. Now that the prospect was looking her in the face, the realization of what was to be sent a dozen razor-sharp knife blades into her belly.

Now she knew how a woman could end up being a man's mistress. She'd always thought it was simply a matter of untamed lust, or something women who were not respectable did. Now she knew better.

She also knew that neither she nor Kellen would entertain such an arrangement. For all her airs and falseness, Fleurette did not deserve that.

What she had not known was how much this would hurt.

Chapter Eighteen

For the remainder of the day Lolly wanted to scream with the anguish flooding her heart. She bit her lip to suppress the choking sobs that rose into her throat. Somehow she had to live through this. She tried to keep her hands busy so she had no time to think. She visited Mr. Tillotsen at the newspaper office, spent an hour and a half scrubbing the gritty surface of her assigned desk and organized the drawers with paper and pencils and her dictionary all within easy reach. Before teatime, she returned to the hotel, climbed the stairs to her airless room and flung open the single window.

The town was quiet in the hot afternoon air. Peaceful, except for the occasional crunch of buggy wheels on the street below. The mockingbird in the park across the street warbled away on a series of variations. Mr. Bodwin's dog, Tanner, lazed in the open doorway of the mercantile and sniffed half-heartedly at Dora Mae Landsfelter's crisp bombazine skirt when she bustled into the store. Lolly watched at the window for Dora Mae's exit, but when she could no longer sit still, she looked around for something to occupy her hands. She decided to rearrange the garments in the armoire.

Black traveling dress. Two fresh white waists with Valenciennes insets. Her sparse collection of plain, simple day dresses. Her good petticoat and extra camisole and the lacy black shawl, draped over a padded hanger. Those few items, along with the blue percale work skirt and muslin blouse she now wore, constituted her entire wardrobe.

Except for one thing—the wedding gown at the bottom of her trunk. It had been her mother's. She had unpacked the delicate dress and hung it up to shed over twenty-nine years of creases and stale air. Then, after Fleurette had confided her delicate condition, Lolly had rewrapped the ivory silk in tissue paper and laid it away again.

Her heart, her entire being had closed in on itself. Her once-upon-a-time hopes were dashed, her spirit crushed as she confronted the lonely prospect of life without Kellen. Every time she thought of it, her insides felt hollow and her chest tightened into a hard knot of pain.

Later, after the colonel and Fleurette had married and Lolly could face it, she would have the wedding gown remade into something more practical. This evening, when the colonel's engagement was to be announced, she would not let one single tear fall.

She headed down the carpeted stairway and walked through the hotel lobby to the shaded veranda outside. The breeze brushed the two tubbed crape myrtle trees at each end, making a soft rustling noise. Someone had hung a small bell on a lower branch, and every so often it made a sweet, silvery sound in the quiet afternoon. It reminded Lolly of the bell on her father's inner office door.

Her breath stopped. That bell had stopped ringing sixteen years ago when news came of Papa's death at Chancellorsville. Lolly had removed the bell the very next morning. She needed no reminder of her duty to carry on her father's work. Besides, it made her mother cry, and taking care of Mama in her weakening condition had now become Lolly's responsibility.

She sank onto the swing cushion, unlaced her shoes and tucked her feet up under her skirt. *Oh, Papa, I have done as you would have wanted. But*

Mama is gone now, and I have sold the newspaper and left Kansas to pursue a dream.

Maybe it was a silly dream. Maybe she should have never given a thought to her own happiness.

But, Papa, I swear to you, I will never do anything to displease you. All my life I will honor you and what you stood for.

She sat up straight. She felt perfectly dreadful inside, pinched and raw, as if a threshing machine had run amok in her belly. Too much lemonade and applejack, perhaps.

Too much thinking about Papa and the past.

Too much Kellen Macready.

"Dora Mae Landsfelter has a new hat," Carrie whispered. "Just look at that fruit salad on top of her head!"

Fleurette emitted a nervous giggle and fluffed out her peach organza with one small white hand. "It needs a banana, don't y'all think?"

Lolly said nothing. Dora Mae's hat was the last thing on her mind. She watched the jovial crowd across the street coalesce into a quiet, attentive audience in front of the gazebo. They were awaiting Mrs. Landsfelter's announcement, just as she and Fleurette and Carrie were.

She tried to keep from searching for Kellen.

Tried not to think about what would happen this evening. And the next, and the next, until church bells rang and Kellen took his new bride home to the beautiful house on Peach Street.

She clenched her hands into fists and hid them in the folds of her skirt.

After the wedding, she would rent Fleurette's room at Mrs. Petrov's boardinghouse. Natasha Petrov was a widow with two young children. Lolly could spoil them and pretend... A ribbon of pain encircled her heart.

Carrie nudged her. "There's Colonel Macready now. My, he looks quite handsome." Her voice sounded curiously flat.

All at once Carrie jerked and sucked in her breath. "Look! There's Orven Tillotsen, across the square. See? In the blue shirt with the white stripes running through it."

White stripes? Lolly stared at Carrie's rapt face. With the "quite handsome" colonel around, why was Carrie focusing on Orven Tillotsen?

Next to her on the swing, Fleurette gave a little cry. "The colonel's lookin' right at us!" She squirmed, then rearranged the folds of her gown to spill over Lolly's plain black skirt.

"Peach is Colonel Macready's favorite color,"

Fleurette murmured. "He told me so this afternoon."

The threshing machine gnashed its way into Lolly's chest. "You spoke with the colonel this afternoon?"

"Just foah a minute, yes. Ah was out walkin' on Peach Street, and that dog of his, Sam, commenced to barkin' and then he chased me until the colonel called him off. He was so very gallant about it all, Ah quite forgave him."

Lolly bit down on her tongue. She didn't want Kellen to be gallant! She wanted him to be—well, she didn't know what. But not gallant.

"Ladies and gentlemen." Dora Mae's voice carried across the street where Lolly sat frozen with Fleurette and Carrie. She could not move even one little finger.

Hank Morehouse lounged on the step below the veranda, a half-eaten apple in one hand. He bit into it just as Dora Mae spoke.

"Shhhh!" Carrie hissed. Hank turned scarlet and stuffed the remains of the apple into his shirt pocket.

Dora Mae raised her arms, signaling for quiet. "The Maple Falls Ladies Helpful Society," she articulated clearly, "has raised the sum of four hundred and thirty-seven dollars, enough to build a new schoolhouse and pay a year's salary to a new schoolteacher, if one is needed.''

Carrie went rigid. "*New* schoolteacher?''

"Course, silly. Married women cain't teach school. Leastways they cain't in N'Awlins.''

"But this is Oregon! *I* want to be the school-teacher!''

"Go raht ahead, sugar. *Ah* want to marry the colonel!''

Lolly wanted to crawl under the swing and put her hands over her ears.

"And now…'' Dora Mae gestured Colonel Macready to her side. "We, that is, the Ladies Helpful Society, have an announcement to— Why, Colonel, whatever are you doing?''

Colonel Macready stepped forward, laid two de-termined hands on Dora Mae's shoulders and gently but purposefully set her to one side.

"*I* have an announcement to make,'' he said when the laughter died down. "Or rather a question to pose. Which,'' he added in the same calm voice, "has not one damn thing to do with the Ladies Helpful Society or the new schoolhouse.''

Applause broke out. Dora Mae's face went slack.

The colonel paused for so long Lolly thought she was going to explode, and then he drew in a long, deep breath. Lolly breathed in along with him. But until he spoke, she couldn't breathe out.

The colonel's mouth opened. Even from here she could see the sheen of perspiration on his forehead.

Lolly clenched her hands and scrunched both eyes shut. She would *not* cry. She would smile and hug Fleurette and be happy for her.

Kellen's low voice floated to her ears as if he were standing right there on the veranda in front of her.

"Miss Leora Mayfield, will you marry me?"

What had he said? *Marry him?*

Lolly's lids popped open in time to see Fleurette slide gracefully out of the swing in a swoon. Carrie threw her arms around her.

"Oh, Leora! Leora! I am so happy for you!"

Lolly tried desperately to remember what for. Oh, yes, the colonel.

The colonel! Wanted to marry *her?*

And Carrie didn't mind?

Fleurette lay like a puddle of peach fluff on the veranda floor, and she...

Oh, no. She was going to faint herself.

Or cry. Maybe both.

Sol Stanton bounded up the hotel steps and knelt beside Fleurette's motionless form. "Miss Le-

Clair." He clasped one of her pale hands. "Miss LeClair, can you hear me?"

Orven Tillotsen stood off to one side, scribbling in his notebook as fast as his pencil would go.

Across the square Lolly met Kellen's eyes, and without another thought she rose unsteadily and let her feet carry her forward to meet him.

They stood a scant foot apart, the raucous crowd roiling around them. It seemed to Lolly that half the men in Maple Falls were pounding Kellen on the back. He leaned toward her.

"Say yes, for God's sake, Leora."

"But…but I thought…"

"I know." Someone shoved him and he brushed against her. His eyes darkened to polished ebony. "I know why you wanted me to marry Fleurette, but I couldn't do it, not after last night with you."

"But… Oh, Kellen, Fleurette *needs* you. She really does, in the most desperate way."

"She will be all right, Leora. Sol Stanton is head over coattails in love with her."

Lolly nodded dumbly, the features of his face blurring as her eyes stung.

"The question is," he said in a hoarse voice, "will *you* be happy?"

"Happy?" The word made no sense way up on the rosy cloud where she drifted.

"With me," he said. A pause. "Married." Another pause. "To me."

"Why are you talking so oddly, just one word at a time?"

"Because I'm scared half to death."

"Kellen, I think you should know something. I have taken over a desk at the newspaper office."

"Should that be a problem?"

"You don't mind?"

He leaned down, spoke against her ear. "That depends."

"D-depends on what?"

He pulled her into his arms. "On whether I—we—are to have a wedding."

Lolly looked up at him through a veil of tears. "Well, of course we are." She licked her lips and composed her next thought.

"I promised Orven Tillotsen I would cover the event for the newspaper."

Chapter Nineteen

Golden Valley Gazette
June 12, 1879

Engagement Announcement Leads to Surprises
Reported by Orven Tillotsen, editor

Such excitement has not been seen in Maple
Falls since Tom Fantini's goat got loose in the
town square and ate all the peonies in the Gundersen Memorial Garden.

Thursday evening Dora Mae Landsfelter,
president of the Maple Falls Ladies Helpful
Society, gathered the townspeople to announce
the engagement of Colonel Kellen Macready.

However, the venerable woman found herself summarily set aside by the forenamed citizen who proceeded to shock those gathered by his public proposal to Maple Falls newcomer Leora Mayfield!

At press time, this reporter was unable to determine Miss Mayfield's answer. Instead, other interesting events occurring at the same time will be reported.

That same evening, Miss Careen Gundersen displayed admirable composure when her young cousin, Hank Morehouse, tripped on a carelessly tossed apple core while descending the steps of the Golden Valley Hotel and broke his arm.

The lovely and intrepid Miss Gundersen instantly retrieved her bottle of lavender salts from her reticule and waved it under the young man's nose until coherent speech returned, then supervised splinting of the limb using rolled-up copies of the *Golden Valley Gazette,* which the enterprising Miss Gundersen gathered from the hotel dining room. Such demonstration of levelheaded pluck under duress is most admirable.

Young Hank's arm is currently encased in plaster.

The next eye-opening event concerns another newcomer to our fair town, Miss Fleurette LeClair, who fainted dead away on the hotel veranda following Colonel Macready's proposal to Miss Mayfield. To the rescue dashed retired railroad magnate Solway Stanton, formerly of Philadelphia. Mr. Stanton revived Miss LeClair and then heroically transported her in his arms the seven blocks to her residence at Natasha Petrov's boardinghouse on Cherryvale Street.

The engagement of Kellen Macready comes as a welcome surprise to this community, which has long wondered when and to whom the much-admired colonel would be affianced. Suffice to say, the expected event follows the Macready family tradition of garnering numerous military and personal honors before settling down.

Colonel Macready's father and grandfather before him were respected political leaders of Hanover County, Virginia, prior to the War between the States, and it was as a direct result of the colonel's brilliant leadership that his troops at Chancellorsville vanquished a troop of Federal soldiers, garnering him three medals of valor for bravery against opposing Union forces.

Colonel Macready and his new bride will reside at his home on Peach Street. The wedding date has not yet been set.

Lolly looked up from the newspaper with a sinking feeling in her chest. Kellen had been at Chancellorsville? *He* had led the Rebel troops against the small band of Union soldiers that had been slaughtered that horrible day? Her father's troops? *How can I possibly marry the man who was responsible for Papa's death?*

"Leora?"

"Fleurette, the night you entertained the colonel, did he talk about the war?"

Fleurette blinked. "About Chancellorsville, yes. He spoke of it at length. Why?"

"There's something about it in the *Gazette*," Lolly said.

"Now you know Ah cain't reveal..." Fleurette glanced about the dining room where they sat. "What does it say?"

"That Kellen was decorated for...for..." She couldn't say the words.

"Of course he was! He is a brave and gallant

man. He must have been eveh so courageous as an officer.''

"Yes," Lolly murmured. "I'm sure he was."

Carrie breezed in, clad in ruffled blue gingham. Her large brown eyes shone. "You'll never guess what!"

Lolly and Fleurette regarded her in silence.

"Orven Tillotsen—'' Carrie stopped, blushed and sank onto the seat opposite them ''—has proposed!''

"Proposed what?" Lolly said absently.

Fleurette's golden eyelashes fluttered shut, then snapped open. "Proposed? As in asked for your hand in—''

"Yes!" Carrie squealed.

"And?" Fleurette and Lolly leaned toward her. "What did you say?"

"I said 'Yes!'''

"That explains the editorial bias in the *Gazette* this morning," Lolly said, trying to smile. "'The lovely and intrepid Miss Gundersen.'''

"Did he say that? Why that sweet, sweet gentleman.''

Leora squeezed her hand. "Congratulations, Carrie. Mr. Tillotsen is a fine man.''

"So," Fleurette uttered in a dreamy voice, "is Mr. Stanton.''

"Sol?" Carrie stood and flung her arms about Fleurette. "Do you fancy Sol?"

"His given name is Edward," Fleurette said softly. "'Sol' is short for Solway, which is his mothah's family name."

"You haven't answered the question," Carrie prodded.

"Well, Ah do rather admire him."

"And he has simply pots of money," Carrie confided. "He invested in railway stock."

Fleurette studied the tablecloth. "He rather admires me, as well. Leastways that's what he said last night after Ah made such a fool of myself."

Carrie jumped to her feet. "You realize what this means?"

Lolly and Fleurette looked at each other. Carrie danced a little jig around the table. "We're *all* going to be married! Each of us! Happy ever after, just like in the fairy stories."

Lolly's throat closed. "Excuse me," she managed. "I don't think I...remembered to..."

She escaped before she finished the sentence.

"Remembered to what?" a suddenly deflated Carrie inquired.

"Forgive herself, sugar. For lovin' the man who killed her father."

* * *

Lolly's hand shook so violently she could hardly grasp the iron knocker. After her second attempt, the glass-paneled door swung open.

"Leora!" Kellen reached out his hand to her. "Come in. Mrs. Squires is so addled at our engagement she can't boil eggs this morning. After you calm her down, I have something special to—"

The instant he touched her, his face changed. "Why, you're shaking! What on earth is wrong?"

Lolly opened her mouth, but nothing came out. She swallowed over her tight and aching throat and tried again. "Kellen…"

"Yes, my darling? What is it?" He touched her cheek, then tipped her face up to his. "Leora, you've been crying."

"Oh, Kellen."

He pulled her into his arms and held her tight. "Tell me," he said in a low voice. "Tell me now."

Lolly gulped back a sob. "I—I can't marry you."

His face went white. "You could yesterday," he said in a puzzled voice. "What has happened?"

Lolly clung to him, buried her face against his linen shirt. "It happened a long time ago," she choked out. "During the war."

"*What* happened during the war?"

"Chancellorsville."

Kellen groaned. "Oh, God. I've spent fifteen years trying to forget that awful day." He smoothed her hair with one hand, kept the other tight across her back. "What about Chancellorsville?"

"My father...my father was..." She could not finish the thought.

His hand lifted from her hair. "Oh, no. Goddammit, no!" His voice was so full of pain Lolly winced.

"I've never been proud of what happened there. Always hated the medals, the newspaper stories. Hated the whole war after that." He fell silent for a long minute. "Your father was there, wasn't he? Oh, God, you must hate me, as well."

Lolly wept against his hard chest until her head hurt and there were no more tears left.

"No, Kellen, I don't hate you." She leaned away from him, brushed the wetness from her eyes with her fingers. "I just...I just can't marry you now. It would betray my father's memory, betray everything he stood for. I swore I would never do that."

"I love you, Leora. I always will."

She broke away, knowing if she did not end it now, she would not be able to do what she must.

"I love you, too, Kellen. But I cannot marry you."

She left him standing on the porch, looking after her, his mouth twisted in anguish.

Hours later, Lolly wrapped her arms over her middle and pushed off on the veranda swing. Back and forth she rocked, trying to think. Trying desperately to stop feeling.

"Leora?"

Lolly stiffened at the softly accented voice. "I am not fit company, Fleurette. Some other time."

Fleurette proceeded up the stairs anyway and glided onto the swing beside her. "Course yoah not fit company. But there *is* no other time. Ah must speak to you. Now."

Lolly laced her fingers into a knot in her lap to hide their trembling. "What is it?"

"Don't you want to know *why* there is no other time?"

She choked back a groan. How Fleurette loved to tease. No matter what was going on, she strung things out because it made her the center of attention.

"No," she said dully, "I do not want to know why."

"Course you do, honey. Yoah just out o' sorts

because of what you read in the *Gazette*. About the colonel, I mean.''

''You are quite right. It is about the colonel.''

''Colonel Macready was a Reb. Yoah daddy was a Yankee.''

Lolly felt her stomach lurch. ''Yes. My father was killed at Chancellorsville. Cut down in his tracks along with twenty other men when the Confederate officer broke through the Union lines. Papa's commanding officer wrote us about it.''

''Leora, that was fifteen years ago.''

''It doesn't matter. That Reb officer was Colonel Macready.''

''Oh, Leora, do grow up!'' Fleurette stopped the motion of the swing and turned to her. ''Ah think it's not so much that Colonel Macready was responsible for yoah father's death as somethin' else.''

Lolly's insides turned to lead. ''What 'something else'?''

''Ah don't have much book-learnin', honey. And you don't know much about men. So you just hush up and listen.''

Lolly stared at the resolute heart-shaped face, the knowing green eyes. Fleurette was right. She didn't know much about men. She knew about newspaper reporting. About truth and justice.

"Ah'm sure yoah daddy was a good man," Fleurette said softly.

Lolly's throat tightened. "Yes, he was."

"And he loved you."

Lolly nodded.

"But, honey, he wasn't perfect, was he?"

"Nobody is perfect. I know that."

"Well, Leora, don't you see? Neither is Colonel Macready."

Her heart did a little rollover inside her chest. Oh, my Lord, all at once she did see. Men, like women, just did the best they could in a given situation. And everyone, at one time or another— even honorable men like Kellen Macready—did things they later wished they hadn't.

How odd that Fleurette should be the one to bring her to her senses, but there it was. She took the young woman's hands in her own. "I do see, Fleurette. Really I do."

"Mah mama always said, 'It's honey that attracts bees, but it's vinegar that soothes the sting.' Ah just spread a little vinegar on yoah hurtin' heart."

"Thank you," Lolly said simply. She squeezed Fleurette's small hands.

"Yoah welcome. Now, Ah do hope you'll forgive me for askin' a favor of you in return."

"Favor? What sort of favor?"

Fleurette swallowed. "After the weddin'—Sol's and mine, that is—weah supposed to sign some sort of form, with writin' on it."

Lolly looked into the troubled green eyes. "Yes, the marriage contract. What about it?"

"Leora, please. Ah want you to teach me to read."

For a moment Lolly wasn't sure she had heard correctly. Fleurette admitted she needed help? *Her* help?

"Oh, my dear, of course I will teach you!"

"By next Sunday?" Fleurette added in a pinched voice.

The two women's gazes caught and held. "By next Sunday," Lolly promised.

And then they were laughing and crying and hugging each other while the swing gently rocked to and fro.

She was halfway across the field of lavender when she caught sight of Kellen's tall form approaching from the opposite direction. Before she had taken another step, Sam frisked at her feet.

"You rambunctious old thing! You've been rolling in the lavender, haven't you? You smell just like my mother's scented sheets!"

Sam rolled over in an ecstasy of delight at her voice, then sprang up to nuzzle her hand with his wet nose. Lolly laughed over the ache in her throat. "My goodness, such devotion!"

She raised her head and watched Kellen approach. He did not speak until he reached her, and then his arms came around her and he held her close. "Leora, I had to see you. I won't give you up, not without a fight. We have to talk this through!"

She nodded, unable to speak.

"I was afraid…" he began.

Lolly laid her fingers against his lips. "I was coming to see you. To tell you…to tell you it will be all right."

"Oh, God, Leora." He caught her close again, pressed his lips into her hair. "I came to beg you on my knees to reconsider."

"I loved my father dearly, Kellen. But I love you, as well. Papa would not wish me to set aside my happiness for an old hurt."

"Leora, now that we have found each other, don't leave me. Ever."

"I will never leave you, Kellen. Don't you know that?"

"No," he rumbled softly against her cheek. "I

.did not know that. How on earth could I have known that?''

She pulled his head down to hers. ''By using your powers of deductive reasoning, of course.'' She kissed one corner of his mouth. ''I love you.''

She kissed the other corner. ''You love me. That's all that is important.''

For some minutes she let her lips and tongue speak for her while Kellen held her close in his arms.

''And besides—'' she looked up at him through tear-blurred eyes ''—my ice cream freezer is in your kitchen.''

''Three weddings in one summer?'' Dora Mae Landsfelter's hands darted to her bosom, narrowly missing her lemonade glass on the table where the four women were gathered. ''I don't know whether Hulda Jane can manage three weddings in one summer.''

''Your daughter-in-law will not be needed,'' Carrie reassured the panting woman. ''I am sewing my own wedding dress.''

''Ah think mah gown will need only a slight bit of alteration—'' Fleurette caught Lolly's eye ''—around the waist.''

Lolly spoke in a voice dazed with happiness.

"And I will wear the gown my mother wore when she married my father. It is ivory silk."

Dora Mae rapped her teaspoon against her glass. "Could we get back to the business at hand, ladies?"

Carrie cocked her head and directed her grin to Dora Mae's new flower-bedecked hat. "What business is that?"

"The receptions, naturally. The Ladies Helpful Society will host your wedding receptions."

"All three of them?" Carrie said, her tone carefully matter of fact.

"Well…"

"All or none," Fleurette said. "Weah togetheh till the end, aren't we?"

"And beyond," Carrie responded. All at once her brown eyes shone with moisture.

Lolly's laugh bubbled out of nowhere. "For better or worse."

Fleurette beamed. "Good. And when y'all stand up as mah bridesmaids, Ah do hope we will not clash."

Carrie and Lolly exchanged a glance. "We wouldn't think of it. Leora is wearing green and purple," Carrie teased with a perfectly straight face. "And I'm wearing chartreuse. Such a lovely color for summer, don't you think?"

Fleurette's cheeks went white as a pillowcase, then turned rose-red. ''Y'all funnin' me, aren't you?''

Lolly and Carrie grinned at each other across the table. ''Wait and see.''

Epilogue

Years later, it was known as the Wedding Cake Summer. For posterity, the *Golden Valley Gazette* recorded the nuptial events as follows.

June 24, 1879

Careen Elizabeth Gundersen and Orven Tillotsen were joined in marriage this past Sunday with the Reverend Arnold Nodding, greatuncle of the bride, performing the ceremony in the Maple Falls First Methodist Church.

The former Miss Gundersen was given away by her father, Otis Gundersen III. The bride's cousin, Henry Morehouse, bore the ring on a white satin pillow.

Attended by Miss Fleurette LeClair and

Miss Leora Mayfield in matching gowns of ice-blue silk, the bride was attired in white peau de soie with lacework at the neck and around the deeply scalloped hem. She carried a bouquet of white roses, candytuft and bridal wreath spirea.

The new Mrs. Tillotsen is the daughter of Otis and Velma Gundersen and served as schoolteacher at the Maple Falls school. The groom is the eldest son of Calvin and Lavinia Tillotsen of Russells Landing (Lane County). Mr. Orven Tillotsen is owner and editor of the *Golden Valley Gazette*.

Following the ceremony a reception was held in the church social hall, hosted by Mrs. Dora Mae Landsfelter and ladies of the Maple Falls Helpful Society. A delicious triple-layer cinnamon-spice wedding cake was served to the guests.

July 7, 1879

Joined in matrimony this day were Fleurette Francine LeClair of New Orleans and Edward Solway Stanton, formerly of Philadelphia, who claimed his bride in a double-ring ceremony held in the town square gazebo.

Radiant in a tiered cream lace gown with lace-capped sleeves and a demi-train, the bride spoke her vows attended by Mrs. Orven Tillotsen, the former Careen Gundersen and Miss Leora Mayfield. Both women were attired in rose-pink brocade with ribbon bows accenting a six-gored skirt and carried bouquets of pink baby tea roses. The bride wore a crown of the same blooms securing a short veil over her hair.

Following the ceremony, the bride and groom accepted the congratulations of well-wishers on the veranda of the Golden Valley Hotel, where a spectacular three-layer white almond cake, a cherished recipe of the bride's grandmother, was served by ladies of the Maple Falls Helpful Society.

The new Mrs. Stanton and her husband will reside at the Stanton mansion on Ash Street. Following their return from a month-long honeymoon journey to Italy, the couple will entertain at home on Thursdays from two until five in the afternoon.

September 1, 1879

Leora June Mayfield, lately of Baxter Springs, Kansas, and Colonel Kellen Macready were wed this past Sunday in the most unusual site ever chosen for a matrimonial pact—the Underwoods' lavender field. The simple ceremony was witnessed by Orven and Careen Tillotsen, Solway and Fleurette Stanton and Mrs. Marjorie Squires.

For her wedding the former Miss Mayfield wore her mother's wedding gown of ivory silk cut on the bias with off-the-shoulder sleeves. She carried a bouquet of purple clematis and lavender. Colonel Macready presented his bride with an amethyst-and-diamond wedding band worn by his great-aunt Henrietta Macready.

Following the ceremony, the wedding party retired to Colonel Macready's elegant home on Peach Street, where townspeople and guests were entertained at a garden reception. A towering three-layer chocolate-rum-walnut wedding cake was served to the delight of all in attendance.

The new Mrs. Macready is a columnist for the *Golden Valley Gazette*. Colonel Macready is a retired military officer and honorary head of the newly formed Maple Falls Croquet Association.

* * *

As to what happened in Maple Falls later that year, which only the farsighted Madge Squires could have predicted, the less said at this point the better. Suffice to say the entire ruckus has been preserved for all time in the pages of the *Golden Valley Gazette*. A write-up of these events will shortly be forthcoming.

* * * * *

Harlequin Historicals®
Historical Romantic Adventure!

IMMERSE YOURSELF IN THE RUGGED
LANDSCAPE AND INTOXICATING
ROMANCE ON THE AMERICAN FRONTIER.

ON SALE NOVEMBER 2004

WYOMING WOMAN by Elizabeth Lane

After attending college back east, Rachel Tolliver
returns to her family's cattle ranch and falls for sheep
rancher Luke Vicente. Will their romance mean disaster
for their feuding families—or can love truly conquer all?

THE WEDDING CAKE WAR by Lynna Banning

Spinster Leora Mayfield answers an ad for a mail-order
bride, only to find she must compete with two other
ladies to wed Colonel Macready. Can baking the perfect
wedding cake win the contest—and the colonel?

ON SALE DECEMBER 2004

THE LAST HONEST LAWMAN by Carol Finch

After witnessing a shooting, Rozalie Matthews is
abducted by wounded outlaw Eli McCain. Framed
for a murder he didn't commit, Eli is desperate to
prove his innocence. Can Roz listen to her heart
and help him—before it's too late?

MONTANA WIFE by Jillian Hart

Rayna Ludgrin faces financial ruin after her
husband's death, until chivalrous neighbor
Daniel Lindsay offers his help—and his hand in
marriage. When their friendship deepens, Rayna
finds love is sweeter the second time around.

www.eHarlequin.com

HHWEST34

Harlequin Historicals®
Historical Romantic Adventure!

TRAVEL BACK TO THE FUTURE
FOR ROMANCE—WESTERN-STYLE!
ONLY WITH HARLEQUIN HISTORICALS.

ON SALE JANUARY 2005

TEXAS LAWMAN by Carolyn Davidson

Sarah Murphy will do whatever it takes to save her nephew
from dangerous fortune seekers—including marrying lawman
Blake Caulfield. Can the Lone Star lawman keep them
safe—without losing his heart to the feisty lady?

WHIRLWIND GROOM by Debra Cowan

Desperate to avenge the murder of her parents, all trails lead
Josie Webster to Whirlwind, Texas, much to the chagrin of
charming sheriff Davis Lee Holt. Let the games begin as
Davis Lee tries to ignore the beautiful seamstress who stirs
both his suspicions and his desires....

ON SALE FEBRUARY 2005

PRAIRIE WIFE by Cheryl St.John

Jesse and Amy Shelby find themselves drifting apart after
the devastating death of their young son. Can they put
their grief behind them and renew their deep and abiding
love—before it's too late?

THE UNLIKELY GROOM by Wendy Douglas

Stranded by her brother in a rough-and-rugged Alaskan
gold town, Ashlynne Mackenzie is forced to rely on the
kindness of saloon owner Lucas Templeton. But kindness
has nothing to do with Lucas's urges to both protect the
innocent woman and to claim her for his own.

www.eHarlequin.com   HHWEST35

If you enjoyed what you just read,
then we've got an offer you can't resist!

Take 2 bestselling
love stories FREE!

Plus get a FREE surprise gift!